"Megan, there is something I can't tell you."

Tyler kept watching the water flow into the lake. "I can only ask you to trust I'm not some kind of villain." He suspected she had heard things about him, or maybe she just wanted to know why he didn't speak of some things.

After a couple passed by, he turned to face her. "People get to know each other by finding out about their past, their likes, dislikes. But there are things I can't talk about yet. More important than where I've been or what I've done is the present. I'm asking you to take me at face value."

Sandy Pines

YVONNE LEHMAN is an award-winning, best-selling author of forty-five books, including mainstream, mystery, romance, young adult, and women's fiction. Recent books are *Carolina*, *South Carolina*, *Coffee Rings*, a novella in the collection *Schoolhouse Brides*, and *Moving the Mountain*. Founder and director of her own writers' conference for seventeen years, she now directs the Blue Ridge Mountains Christian Writers Conference held annually at the Ridgecrest/LifeWay Conference Center near Asheville, NC.

Books by Yvonne Lehman

HEARTSONG PRESENTS

Don't miss out on any of our super romances. Write to us at the following address for information on our newest releases and club information.

Heartsong Presents Readers' Service
PO Box 721
Uhrichsville, OH 44683

Or visit www.heartsongpresents.com

By Love Acquitted

Yvonne Lehman

Heartsong Presents

A note from the Author:
I love to hear from my readers! You may correspond with me by writing:

Yvonne Lehman
Author Relations
PO Box 721
Uhrichsville, OH 44683

ISBN 978-1-59789-509-5

BY LOVE ACQUITTED

All scripture quotations are taken from the HOLY BIBLE, NEW INTERNATIONAL VERSION®. NIV®. Copyright © 1973, 1978, 1984 by International Bible Society. Used by permission of Zondervan. All rights reserved.

All of the characters and events in this book are fictitious. Any resemblance to actual persons, living or dead, or to actual events is purely coincidental.

Our mission is to publish and distribute inspirational products offering exceptional value and biblical encouragement to the masses.

PRINTED IN THE U.S.A.

one

"Guilty, Your Honor."

Although he was innocent of all charges, that was the only answer Tyler Corbin had insisted on giving when the judge asked, "How do you plead?"

The rest was history—a history Tyler wondered if he would ever forget. Now—two years later—Tyler was finding he couldn't get enough of the fresh spring air, the mountain scenery, the sky, the feeling of freedom. A gleeful laugh broke free from his lips.

Penny Corbin glanced at him and smiled. She turned off the main road and onto the more deserted one leading to their home.

"Oh, Tyler," she said. "I haven't seen you look so happy in. . ." She blinked to clear the moisture in her blue eyes. "I guess since before Mom and Dad died."

He shook his head, aware of how carefully his nineteen-year-old sister was driving. Probably to overcompensate for the past. "Penny, I thought I knew how to appreciate freedom, these mountains, everything. But it's true that you don't really know what you have until you lose it."

Penny nodded. "Like Mom and Dad." Her tone of voice lowered with affection. "And you."

He reached over and tugged on her blond ponytail. "You haven't lost me."

She swiped at a tear. "How can I ever repay you?"

He scoffed. "You already have, by becoming the accomplished

young lady that you are. And, Penny, that was my choice. It's over. I don't even want to discuss it. You know the saying, 'Today is the first day of the rest of your life.' That's how I feel. Sort of. . .reborn."

He saw an intriguing sight ahead. "Uh-oh. Slow down."

The intriguing sight was not the red sports car with the hood up, parked on the side of the road, but the redheaded woman in a tailored navy blue suit, doing a most unladylike thing. The toe of her high-heeled shoe kicked the tire, and he thought it likely a good thing he couldn't read lips. "Pull off ahead of her, Penny."

Penny steered the car to the side of the road. "Always the chivalrous knight," she said. "Helping ladies in distress."

Only once. Tyler opened the car door. But he didn't expect this time to result in his spending two years in prison. He paused and looked at Penny. "Come with me." He couldn't chance anything happening that his parole officer might misconstrue on his first day out of prison.

He stepped onto the shoulder, thick with overgrown grass and weeds. For the first time in his life he empathized with people who kissed the ground when returning to a beloved place after having been away. Grass, weeds, mud, whatever— he loved and appreciated them all after walking mainly on concrete for two years. The way he felt brought back the memory of when he was ten years old, delighting in Penny's taking her first baby steps. Almost giddy with gratitude now, he would never again take for granted the simple acts of walking on mountain soil and reaching out to touch a long-stemmed weed, as he was doing.

With Penny beside him, he neared the woman. "Have a flat tire?" He wasn't sure he remembered how to change one.

He'd done that with the help of buddies in high school about a decade ago.

"No. My tires—" The woman stopped talking suddenly. A look of chagrin passed over her flushed face, causing her cheeks to redden deeper.

Red. How many shades of red could there be? Her hair was nowhere near as bright as the car. He supposed her hair would be called auburn, with the sun giving it a reddish-gold sheen. Her brown eyes glinted with golden sparks he suspected were due to frustration.

"Oh, you must have seen me kick the tire." The shake of her head caused her hair to fall forward toward her face, partially shielding it.

Tyler shrugged and lifted his eyebrows in a noncommittal gesture.

Penny laughed. "That works for me. Kicking or hauling off and walloping an appliance makes it behave every time."

The pretty woman managed a smile. "I'm not sure a kick or a wallop will work on my engine light." Her soft golden-brown gaze fell on Tyler, and he felt as if it were a magnet, drawing him to her. Mentally shaking away the feeling, he walked to the raised hood. Of course he understood this. In the past twenty-four months his view of females had been as limited as vision on a foggy morning here in the mountains of western North Carolina. His association had mainly been with guys in jeans and light blue shirts with numbers on them. He'd had minimal glimpses of female office workers, a few women who performed at special religious programs, an occasional female attorney, and prison nurses who could wield a mean needle.

But he suspected a light sprinkling of freckles across a

perfectly formed nose would be appealing anytime. He kept his eyes on the cap he was unscrewing, however, lifted the dipstick, and felt he could accurately diagnose the problem. "This is likely your problem. No oil. Without it your engine can lock up." He dared a glance at her. "Were you able to drive off the road all right?"

She nodded. "I pulled over when the engine light came on. I don't know a lot about cars, but I know that's a danger sign. I've called the police and my auto insurance company."

He saw she held a cell phone. *Smart girl, keeping her phone in her hand while on the side of the road alone.* This was one of the safest areas anywhere, though, but that didn't mean something unusual couldn't occur.

"We can get oil for you," Penny offered.

Tyler agreed. "Since the engine didn't lock up, maybe that's all you need."

She looked at her wristwatch. "What I need is to get up the mountain—"

Her words stopped when a police car pulled up in back of the red sports car.

Oh, no! On his first day of freedom a policeman was the last person he wanted to see.

When the policeman drew nearer, Tyler thought he looked familiar, but not one who had arrested him after the accident.

"Megan McKinney?" the policeman said. He glanced at Tyler and Penny.

"That's me," Megan said. Tyler thought her name as pretty as she was. "These two stopped to help me."

This seemed the right time for introductions. "Tyler Corbin." He glanced at his sister. "This is Penny Corbin."

The policeman nodded. "I'm Bill Probe." He took another

look at Tyler. "Corbin? You went to Owen High, didn't you? A year ahead of me." He looked thoughtful. "Yeah. You were one of the smart ones, if I remember right—president of"—he shrugged—"something."

Tyler smiled. "And you were the football quarterback starting your junior year."

Bill laughed. "Oh, yeah. Remember that championship game with Reynolds? Man—" He stopped suddenly and changed the subject. "But I guess remembering's not what we're here for."

Tyler hoped not, but he could almost see the wheels turning in Bill's brain. He knew the cop was remembering something else. "You're—" He stopped there, but Tyler thought he was about to add, "Out."

"I'm back," Tyler said. He looked off at the pine trees on the other side of the road.

Bill turned to Megan. "So what seems to be your problem?"

Megan told him Tyler's assessment and that Penny and Tyler offered to get oil for her.

Bill took it upon himself to check it out and agreed that lack of oil was likely the problem.

"Excuse me," Megan said. "I have to make two phone calls. I'll call the auto company and tell them not to come unless I call again. And I have to call the Campbells up the mountain. I'm a Realtor, and I'm supposed to list their property. Now I'm late."

"Oh, I know the Campbells," Penny said. "We'll take you up there, go get your oil, then pick you up." She looked at Tyler. "Right, Tyler?"

Tyler cast a glance Penny's way. "Sure," he said, but he wasn't sure if that was the best or the worst of ideas.

❧

Megan made her calls while the policeman lowered the hood on her car. She watched as he spoke a few words to the other two, then lifted his hand in farewell. Megan smiled and nodded, so he walked back to the police car. After getting her briefcase and locking her car, Megan followed Penny and Tyler to the little black car.

"Thank you," she said, slipping into the passenger seat while Tyler held the door. He nodded and closed it, then slid into the backseat. The thought occurred to Megan that when a man and woman rode together the man usually drove. But that was no hard, fast rule.

Fastening her seat belt, Megan thought of the statement that some good comes from the worst of things. Only an instant passed before she felt a smile coming to her lips. Yes, her car trouble had resulted in the rare occurrence of her meeting two intriguing men—in one day—who looked to be about her age of twenty-eight. Neither wore a wedding band, but that didn't always mean anything. The pleasant, nice-looking cop had been a high school football hero. The tall one in the backseat was someone she, in her five-foot-eight-inch frame, could literally look up to. This one, whom the policeman described as a "smart one, president of something" was quite handsome with wheat-colored hair and interesting blue-gray eyes. He was chivalrous to have stopped to help. But he had a young woman with him, who also was not wearing a wedding band or engagement ring; yet they had the same last name. She supposed *Corbin* wasn't all that uncommon, though. And, too, most men her age were married or divorced and dating a younger woman.

Yet she thought these two resembled each other. Or maybe

that was some hope she'd tried to put to rest—that a man was out there somewhere for her. She reminded herself she was quite content in being independent and making her own living without depending upon a man. But that didn't keep her from being aware of an attractive man when she saw one.

She warned herself her interest in this man who was "back" should be of a spiritual nature, not anything else. Yet she wondered what kind of occupation a "smart one" would have. She should not be wondering if he, sitting behind her, liked her hairstyle that was feathered rather short in back and longer in front with strands falling forward at her chin line and against the sides of her face.

She had a job to do, a car to get running, and clients to meet. She looked over and returned Penny's smile. The girl pulled onto the road and headed up and around the mountain.

Trying to get her mind in gear for business, Megan mentioned the Campbells. "You said you know the Campbells, Penny?"

"Well, I know them to speak to. They live in our neighborhood. Mr. Campbell had heart surgery, and now they're going to Kansas to live with their daughter, who's a nurse. Oh." Penny pointed to the right. "There's where we live. The two-story with the white columns."

"Nice," Megan said, knowing the houses in this neighborhood were upper-middle class. Most were one-story brick ranch with a little pizzazz. A few were two-story with a lot of pizzazz, such as columns, bay windows, and upper balconies. Impeccable landscaping on each house's one-acre lawn formed a perfect picture, although April was still a little early for planting spring flowers.

Penny turned onto a side street. "The Campbells live at the

end. So my brother and I will go get the oil, bring it back, get you, and take you down to the car, and he can pour in the oil." Her ponytail swung around as she faced Megan, then looked at the road again.

"My brother and I?" Megan turned in the seat and smiled at Tyler. "I hate to put you out. I don't know how long this will take."

"Doesn't matter," he said, his gaze holding hers.

Megan quickly turned toward the front again, causing her hair to brush against her cheeks which for some strange reason felt rather warm. She unfastened her seat belt as Penny parked in the driveway. Seeing movement, she noticed an elderly woman had come out onto the porch and lifted her hand in greeting. Megan reached for the handle as Tyler opened the car door and stood back for her to exit.

She swung her legs around, stepped out, and stood, looking up into those blue-gray eyes that seemed to peer into her heart. She lowered her head, searched her purse, and brought out her car keys. "Here. Why don't you go ahead and get the oil and find out if that's the problem? It will save us time after I'm through here."

"What kind of oil do you use?"

Kind of oil? Her mind seemed befuddled, as if someone had poured oil into it.

"That's okay," he said. "You don't have to use the same brand of oil all the time. But I have a question. Are you sure you want to give strangers your car keys? That's a mighty fine-looking sports car."

She looked into those probing eyes again. "Well," she said, lifting her chin. "The policeman trusted you two enough to let you bring me up here. And besides"—she tilted her head and laughed lightly—"I know where you live."

With a slight nod he lifted his hand, palm up, and she dropped the keys into it. She watched as he turned and slid onto the seat where she had sat.

Oh, my. Megan turned and walked swiftly in her high-heeled pumps up the walkway toward the woman on the porch. What was wrong with her? She didn't trust men. But she had not only given her keys to Tyler Corbin, she had actually flirted with him.

two

Tyler watched as Megan walked onto the Campbells' porch and shook hands with the older woman. Then they went inside.

"She's pretty," Penny said.

Wrinkling his brow, Tyler turned his face toward Penny. "Who? Mrs. Campbell?"

Penny hit his arm playfully. "You know who I mean. Megan McKinney."

"Oh, and who are you now? Miss Matchmaker?"

She lifted her chin saucily. "Well, she looked like a pretty good match to me. And I think she likes you."

Tyler had thought so when Megan had turned in the seat to smile at him. Two years ago he would have taken that as interest and an invitation to pursue things. Now everything, including him, was different. He'd have to take things slowly, make his appearance into the community again, and find out how people felt about him.

Penny backed the car out of the driveway. "When we go back, you should ask her out."

Tyler watched his sister looking closely at the road as she headed back down the mountain. "Penny, do you realize I haven't even set foot in the house yet? I have to get acclimated to society again."

Penny wasn't letting it go. "That's why you have to hurry. You've been out of touch too long."

She sure had a point there. But for now he just wanted to enjoy this sense of freedom—to breathe in the mountain air fresh with a piney scent and bask in the spring sunshine falling across his bare forearms as the car wove around the road bordered by tall evergreens.

Soon Penny turned onto the main road. "We can go to Franklin's. That's where I get my car inspected and my oil changed."

She traveled along Highway 70, turned down the road by the depot, now a craft store, crossed the railroad tracks, and drove a couple of more blocks to Franklin's. An incredulous thought jarred Tyler's memory. "Penny, I only have a couple of ones and some change."

His sister's smile complemented the sparkle in her eyes. "I'll get it." She parked on the concrete in front of Franklin's where cars were pulled into the bays and checked. This place was new. Something else new was his sister, ten years younger than he, making a purchase of oil for a car while he sat in the passenger's seat, waiting. Would he even remember how to drive a car? He needed to slow his mind down, as he'd just told Penny, and get acclimated again.

After purchasing the oil, Penny drove them back to Megan's car. Tyler unlocked the door, pulled the lever for the hood, walked around to open it, and unscrewed the cap. He poured in the oil. "Now for the big test." He gestured toward Penny. "You do the honors."

Penny slid into the driver's seat and turned the key in the ignition, and the motor roared to life. She rolled the window down and leaned out the window. "Should I drive it up to the Campbells'?"

That didn't seem like a good idea to Tyler. "No, just drop

me off at the house; then you can bring Megan back down to her car."

Penny huffed. "Tyler, that's not the way to get acquainted with a female."

"Penny," he returned, "neither is being escorted all over the mountain by one's sister."

"Of course not." She slapped her forehead. "I know. You can drop me off at the house, and you bring her down."

"No." Two years ago he likely would have done exactly that. But right now he didn't have his driver's license with him, had very little money, and probably smelled of prison showers.

No, this was much too soon to strike up a relationship with anyone. And he'd have to win someone over, which seemed a long shot, considering how quickly Clare had changed her mind about him—even though she'd known him for over a year and they both taught at the same school. He'd have to prove himself worthy of a woman. That wouldn't be easy, considering he was an ex-con on parole.

❧

Megan knew when the small, black car pulled into the Campbells' driveway. She finished up as quickly as she could, without seeming to rush the older couple. After about ten more minutes, she had a signed listing and bade them good-bye.

When she reached the car she glanced into the backseat. She should not feel disappointed Tyler hadn't come with Penny to take her back down the mountain. Her interest in him was out of curiosity only, of course. Recently having left her home in Charlotte because of a man, she certainly wasn't going to jump into another relationship, and why was she even thinking about such a thing anyway? Well, because she was a red-blooded American girl who recognized an appealing man when she saw one. She also recognized an appealing piece of double-chocolate fudge cheesecake but knew better than to eat much of that.

So the same with men! Admire as yummy. . .then resist.

She did resist asking why Tyler didn't come with Penny to the Campbells' home. After all, it was obvious. He had better things to do.

"Did the oil do the trick?" Megan asked after opening the passenger door and settling into the seat.

Penny's ponytail bobbed as she nodded. "It started, and the engine light went off, so we assume it will be okay." She backed out onto the road and headed back down the mountain.

Megan hoped they were right. "I appreciate this so much, Penny." She opened her purse. "How much do I owe you?"

"Not a cent. It's not worth mentioning." Penny smiled. "I'm sure you'd do the same for anyone stranded on the side of the road."

"I hope so," Megan said. She looked at the house Penny had pointed out as theirs earlier. She realized now that Tyler might even have a wife. Just because he and Penny were brother and sister didn't negate the marital status with someone else.

But she should keep her mind where it belonged. "Penny, do you go to church around here?"

"First Church on Montreat Road."

"Really?" Megan stared at her. "That's where I go. I don't think I've seen you there."

"Well, that's my church as far back as I remember, and I'm a member there. But I've been living in a dorm at Western Carolina University and attending church in Cullowhee. Right now I'm on spring break. I was there last Sunday for the first time in a long time. I'm in the college class."

"That explains it. I've only been there a few months. I'm in the singles' class. All ages." Megan laughed. "But they've already put me to work on the outreach committee. That means I'm to invite every single person I meet to our class." She paused and cleared her throat. "Is your. . .um, Tyler. . . single?"

Penny's laugh was adorable, and Megan had the feeling not much passed by her. The younger girl gave her a sideways glance full of mischief. "As single and as eligible as they get. And it's time. . .um, Tyler. . .got back in church."

Penny used the same inflection in her voice as Megan had with the "um, Tyler," indicating the girl suspected Megan was asking more than if he went to church.

Penny pulled off ahead of Megan's car and cut the engine, giving the keys to Megan. "Do you have family here, Megan?"

Megan nodded. "My aunt Eva. She needed someone after her husband died. And I needed someone. So we make a great team."

A slight sadness crossed Penny's eyes. "It's good to have family. Tyler's all I have. Well, you'd better see if the oil stayed where it was supposed to."

Megan reached for the door handle. "Oh, I never thought there might be a leak." She hastened out, looked under her car, and saw no evidence of leakage. She pushed the remote to unlock the door, then tentatively tried the key in the ignition.

The engine caught. She rolled down the window and stuck her head out, as Penny was doing in her car. "Ah, success! Thank you so much, Penny. Tell Tyler thanks, too."

"You might need to tell him yourself, if you're going to invite him to. . .um, church." She laughed.

Megan shook her head. Young people! At least, if she'd

been interested in pursuing a relationship, the sister seemed to approve. Megan waved, turned the car, and started toward town. In the rearview mirror she saw Penny's car headed up the mountain.

The basket of fruit on the passenger side floor caught her eye. When she got a listing or made a sale, she gave a gift, usually flowers or fruit. She picked up plain, inexpensive baskets and colored cellophane wrap from a craft store in Asheville and bought in-season fruit from the Farmers' Market or Fresh Market. Full of fresh fruit, the basket made a nice gift.

She'd brought a basket of fruit with her in case the Campbells signed. But she owed Tyler and Penny more than verbal thanks, particularly since Penny hadn't taken any money for the oil. The only thing to do was turn around and head back up the mountain, which she did.

≈

Tyler stood when Megan walked up the few steps and stopped between the columns that rose from the porch up to the small balcony. Her glance took in his appearance. He had changed from the casual slacks and short-sleeved sport shirt he'd had on earlier. Now light blue denims hugged his legs. The white knit shirt with a navy stripe across his wide chest revealed broad shoulders and biceps of a man who had spent time in a gym. A faint scent of cleanliness and a musky aftershave tantalized her senses.

It dawned on her he had apparently showered, shaved, and changed clothes. She didn't think men shaved in the late afternoon or evening unless they were going out.

Her gaze lifted to meet his blue-gray one, and she felt the slow crawl of adrenaline course up her spine and knew it would eventually color her cheeks. She was behaving like a girl Penny's age or younger instead of her own age.

Tyler braced his hand on the column. "Uh-oh," he said. "Now you're having a problem with your fruit basket."

Megan stared for a moment; then they both laughed. His humor brought her back to her senses, she hoped.

He stepped back and motioned to a white rocking chair. "Have a seat," he offered.

She eased into the rocker next to where he had been sitting; then he sat. *He's a gentleman, too.* She looked out ahead of her at the pines across the road, the long drive leading to another fine home, and mountains in the distance. "What a beautiful view."

He nodded. "I've been admiring it."

They sat in comfortable silence for a moment, enjoying the view. But she needed to get on with her business and not delay him if he were going out. "I brought this fruit as a thank-you gift for you and Penny. I really appreciate your help."

She stood and handed him the basket.

"Thank you."

Hearing a sound, she looked over to see Penny step onto the porch. She was wearing an apron over her clothes. "Hi, Megan. I thought I heard someone out here. I'm just starting to fix supper. Want to join us?"

Well, maybe Tyler wasn't dressed to go out. Maybe someone was coming here. "Thanks, but Aunt Eva is expecting me for supper. I just brought by a fruit basket as a thank-you gift to you and Tyler."

Penny walked out and picked up the fruit basket from Tyler's lap. "Oh, great. Tyler, this will be our fruit for supper—and dessert."

"Sounds good to me." He smiled.

Megan returned his smile. "Well, I'd better go."

"Did you invite him to. . .um, church?" Penny asked with that look of mischief in her eyes again.

Megan gave her a sly glance. "I was just getting ready to."

Penny winked and carried the basket into the house.

Megan took a deep breath, looking into Tyler's questioning eyes. "I'd like to invite you to my Sunday school class. It's the singles' class at First Church. Penny said that's where she attended before she started college."

Tyler nodded. She thought a sadness passed over his eyes. "That's our home church. Thanks for the invitation." He smiled. This time it didn't seem to reach his eyes. "And for the fruit. Glad your car is okay. Oh, by the way, did you get the listing for the Campbells?"

"Yes, yes, I did." She would love to stay and converse with him. But she'd already refused a supper invitation. Besides, Penny was the one who had offered it.

"Well, thanks again." She lifted her hand in farewell.

All the way to the car she wondered if he was watching her. If so, what did he think? That she was a religious fanatic? That she was doing her Christian duty but didn't really care about him as a person? *Oh, mercy.* She had many more questions than answers. She started the car, turned it around at the side of the house, and looked at the porch before heading down the driveway.

He lifted his hand. Megan smiled and waved.

She hoped she wouldn't weave back and forth or run off the side of the road, knowing he probably was still watching her. Not that it mattered. People around here—especially those rocking on their front porches—watched people.

He was just someone who had done her a great favor. There was nothing personal because she would not allow anything personal from anyone for a long, long time. . .if ever.

To prove to herself she was in control of her actions, emotions, and thoughts, she called her aunt to say she was running late but would be home after a quick visit to the floral shop. She ordered flowers to be sent to the Campbells and wrote a thank-you note. That done, she headed for Aunt Eva's white frame house on Montreat Road.

On her way into the kitchen from the back door, Megan retrieved a basket from the pantry. Aunt Eva was in the spacious kitchen preparing supper. "Sorry I'm later than usual."

"No problem," Aunt Eva said in her usual mild-mannered tone. Megan often wondered how this woman could be in her family but be so different in temperament. Megan had grown up with a very outspoken mother and sister. "When you called and said you might be late I supposed you were showing property."

"I did get another listing." She opened the refrigerator and took fruit from the bin. "I didn't want you to worry, but when I called, I was stranded on the side of the road."

Aunt Eva stopped slicing the tomatoes for the salad. "Oh, Megan. Well, I'm glad you're all right."

Megan told her the story.

"Corbin?" Aunt Eva asked. "I don't know any Corbins personally, but I've heard the name." After remaining thoughtful for a moment she shrugged. "But I can't remember where."

While her aunt put food on the table, Megan made the fruit basket. She added a few more apples, oranges, and grapes than usual. Aunt Eva had a bag of butterscotch crèmes. "Throw in a few of these," she told her.

Megan did and then covered the basket with clear, green-tinted wrap and tied the top with a little green ribbon.

As they sat down to dinner, Aunt Eva said she supposed the basket was for the Campbells.

"No, I sent them flowers." She told about giving the other fruit basket to Tyler and Penny.

"Corbin?" Aunt Eva said.

"Yes."

"And you said he's a nice-looking, single man?"

"Mmm-hmm."

"Hmm," Aunt Eva said and grinned.

Megan figured that "hmm" was because the fried chicken tasted good, but to make sure, she said Bill Probe seemed to be a nice man, too, and he wasn't wearing a ring. That may or may not mean he was married.

"That's who this fruit basket is for," she said. "After supper I want to go to the police station and give Bill the thank-you fruit basket and invite him to church."

"I suppose you invited Tyler Corbin to church?"

"Yes," Megan said. "I did."

The two had talked about their feelings of having to live without someone they loved —the changes, the adjustments. Megan had said she expected a long time to pass before she would ever trust a man again.

Now Aunt Eva looked across at Megan and smiled kindly. She would know Megan wasn't ready for anything personal with a man. "Inviting those men to church is a good thing, dear."

Megan wondered if her aunt was remembering having said she had a good marriage but never wanted another man in her life. Megan had identified with those sentiments exactly, but for different reasons from Aunt Eva's.

three

"For the last time, Penny, I'm not going to that singles' class. I have to do things my way."

Penny held up her hands in surrender. "Okay, okay. But at least come to the worship service. We can sit together."

Tyler laid down the newspaper he'd been reading and was impressed anew with the appearance she made. She looked so pretty and grown-up, with her blond curls around her shoulders. Her blue dress with a short-sleeved jacket made her eyes look blue as a Carolina sky on a clear day. He'd sacrificed those two years so she would have a better life. He wasn't about to do anything to put a damper on that now if he could help it. This would be her last Sunday home before returning to school. Any other time, their sitting together might seem like family togetherness. But not now. He had to readjust without leaning on his nineteen-year-old sister.

"Just do what you normally do, Penny. Don't you eat out with friends on Sunday?"

"Usually," she admitted. "But you're my brother, Tyler. We haven't had anything other than visits in a room full of other people and guards watching us. I have to be back at Western by Wednesday." She paused. "Unless you want me to stay here. I can drive back and forth to my classes."

Tyler scoffed. "An hour and forty-five minutes each way? Penny, I don't want you changing your life for me."

Her blue eyes glistened with moisture. "You did for me."

24

"With no payback," he said. "So don't even try."

Still wearing his pajamas, he stood and opened his arms to her. She came into them. "Penny, I don't even want to think about the past. I'm starting over. Don't keep reminding me. Please."

"I'm sorry," she said against his chest. "I love you so much, Tyler. I want the best for you." She moved back. "And I guess I want it instantly."

He nodded and tugged on one of her curls. It fell back into place as he let it go. "We all want the best, Penny. And instantly. But life isn't that way. We each find our own way or make our own way." He gazed at her a moment longer, then said, "With the Lord's help."

That seemed to make her feel better, and a smile spread across her face. "I'd better go, or I'll be late. And I'll try to quit nagging you."

"Do!" he said. "Otherwise you're going to make some man a terrible wife."

She wrinkled her nose and punched him on the arm.

Tyler stared at the empty doorway long after she left. He loved that girl. They now had the kind of relationship he'd wanted with her after their parents died and he had custody. That had worked for a few months when her shock and grief had been so great. Then she began to change. He hadn't been able to help her.

His two-year sacrifice of his life for hers had been well worth it. He just had to be careful not to let her try to repay him.

Almost an hour later Tyler drove out of the garage in the luxury car that had belonged to his parents. After their deaths he gave his car to Penny, thinking a girl in high school shouldn't be driving around in a new or a luxury car. She threw a fit about it, knowing their parents had a big insurance policy and the house was almost paid for. He'd paid it off and given Penny a healthy allowance. He put the rest in the bank. There was plenty for her college tuition anywhere she wanted to go and maybe a new car when she started college. But Penny had screamed "unfair" and wanted everything instantly, claiming that since she'd lost her parents she should at least have something she wanted.

He had only been trying to be responsible. She understood that now. But he needed to follow his own advice and stop thinking about the past. He found a parking place in the last row at the side of the church. He didn't see a little red sports car. He looked into the rearview mirror and tugged at the knot in his tie as if it had gone askew. Of course it hadn't. And the blue silk matched the color of his summer suit he hadn't worn in over two years. It felt a wee bit snug across the shoulders but had seemed to look fine. This was only for an hour anyway; then he could take it off.

Pastor Wrend stood in the foyer talking with Jim Bishop, whom Tyler had known as a church leader about his dad's age. The pastor's words stopped in midsentence when he saw Tyler. He rushed forward with open arms. "Tyler, Tyler. How good to see you." He hugged Tyler heartily. Holding his Bible in one hand, he returned the embrace. They stepped away. "I knew you were coming soon," he said enthusiastically. "Why didn't you let me know?"

Tyler shook his head. "I just wanted to take things easy for a few days, Pastor." He had made Penny promise not to mention when he'd be home. He hadn't wanted anyone to feel obligated to come to see him. The day after his release he'd checked in with his parole officer and set things up to begin community service at the juvenile center for boys on Monday. Then he'd rocked on the front porch, eating fruit and thinking about a pretty woman in a red sports car. He thought of what could have been, before the events of the last two years, but probably never would be now.

The pastor turned to Jim. "Jim, you remember Tyler Corbin?"

"Certainly," Jim said. He extended his hand, and Tyler shook it. That was a nice gesture. But the man's eyes seemed to hold the kind of question that likely would have been in Tyler's own eyes under the circumstances, and that was, *"Are you a threat to our young people?"*

Tyler didn't want to be any more judgmental of Jim Bishop than he wanted people to be of him. He knew more was expected of Christians than of the world—and rightly so. Christians had God's Word and the Holy Spirit within them to guide them. People who claimed Christ's name had no excuses for deliberate wrongdoing. He expected to be held to that higher standard.

Others were coming into the foyer. "I'd better find a seat," he said, and Pastor Wrend nodded. Jim Bishop handed him a church bulletin, and Tyler thanked him.

Tyler knew he wasn't guilty but figured those who knew where he'd been the past two years would certainly think he was. He looked for an inconspicuous seat, not wanting to attract any undue attention. He reminded himself he was there to worship the Lord and get himself back into the mainstream of life. He mustn't allow his returning to church be because Megan or Penny invited him, but simply because it was the right thing to do.

Apparently Sunday school wasn't over yet. Very few sat in the sanctuary, and he had his choice of seats. There were three aisles. He chose a pew on the far left from where he went in, next to the tall, narrow windows that reached from about waist height to near the cathedral ceiling. The white wooden shutters on the inside were open, letting in the soft spring sunlight. He knew if there were a glare on the congregation someone would shut them.

He gazed out the window, admiring the trees and houses, the clear blue sky, and the few fluffy clouds dotting the horizon. He thought he'd never get enough of open spaces again.

A movement at the front of the sanctuary brought his attention back inside. A screen came down from above the choir loft. Typed announcements began to roll across the screen. That was new for this conservative, traditional church.

He read about what was going on with the church, from babies to senior citizens, a found earring that was in the church office, and an invitation for visitors to go to the fellowship hall for after-service coffee. That, too, was new. Pastor Wrend or someone had made a few changes.

Apparently Sunday school was over. People began streaming into the sanctuary. Penny came in through a doorway down front with a couple of girls. With happy looks on their faces, they were talking. Her gaze scanned the sanctuary, but she didn't see him. Likely she didn't expect him to be there.

He wondered if Megan sang in the choir. About that time he saw her come through the doorway on the far right. She looked relaxed and even more beautiful than a few days ago. Light touched her hair, giving it that reddish-gold sheen. She wore a red, short-sleeved suit with a silky-looking white blouse underneath. He didn't know much about jewelry but thought that thick, gold necklace with a round circle in the middle set everything off perfectly. She lifted her hand to gesture toward a pew, and he noticed she wore a thick gold bracelet.

Wow! She was gorgeous. She and two other classy-looking women slid into the pew. They spoke and smiled at those around them. She didn't see him either. He felt he was fairly well hidden by now. Just as he thought that, he was startled by a voice at his side.

"Okay if I sit by you?"

Tyler turned his head. In the aisle, between him and the window, stood none other than Bill Probe. Bill looked uncomfortable in a gray suit that appeared tighter than Tyler's felt. His curly hair looked a bit windblown, and his tie was askew. Tyler liked being at the end of the row where he could prop his arm on the edge of the pew or look out the window if he wanted. He felt like saying, "No, you can't sit by me," but the hopeful look on Bill's face made him change his mind.

He wouldn't dare stand to let Bill pass by him. They'd likely get stuck. Tyler said, "Sure," and slid over. *Now this must make a pretty sight—the jailbird and the cop sitting together.* Another thought occurred to Tyler. Was Bill keeping tabs on him? If so, surely he wouldn't be so obvious.

Tyler warned himself not to resort to that kind of thinking. He wanted others to accept him for what he was, not what they thought he had been. Then he'd better be willing to accept others. He looked over at Bill, who seemed ill at ease. He was about to ask how long he'd been coming to this church when Phil Jones, the music director, asked everyone to stand and sing the chorus that was printed on the screen.

Bill didn't sing, but Tyler did. Then they were asked to shake hands with those around them. Friendly greetings permeated the sanctuary as people moved around, laughed, and talked.

Bill and Tyler shook hands. Tyler faced the front again and saw a hand reach out on his right. That was a young boy, followed by the hand of a woman and a man he didn't know. The people in front of him turned and shook his and Bill's hands.

No one he knew shook their hands. Maybe that was because they weren't near. Or maybe anyone who knew him didn't care to shake his hand. He forced that thought away, reminding himself how destructive such thinking could be.

The chaplain at the prison had been good, his messages primarily of redemption, change, and inner freedom. There'd been some excellent music groups. But Tyler feared he'd tear up, being here in his home church, hearing the preacher in a different, more mature way than he had all his life. Feeling free in a way some of his prison buddies would never feel. Thank God for inner freedom. That made things bearable.

Tyler shared his Bible and hymnal with Bill. When he pulled from his Bible an old tithe envelope containing his check, Bill took money from his wallet and put it in the collection plate as it was passed.

After the service ended, although the announcement had been printed on the screen earlier, the pastor invited all visitors and anyone who wanted to join them in the fellowship hall. "You going?" Bill asked.

"I hadn't planned to," Tyler said.

Bill shrugged. "I will if you will."

"Sure," Tyler said. He figured, why not? Already he thought the jailbird and the cop, looking buddy-buddy, would make good after-church conversation.

four

"I have a sneaking suspicion your favorite color is red."

Megan recognized Tyler Corbin's voice. She dropped her plastic stirring stick into her Styrofoam cup of coffee into which she'd just poured powdered creamer. Telling herself to keep her cool, she stirred. "How did you ever guess?" She picked up the cup. "Is red your favorite color?"

"It is now."

She hoped he liked it in cheeks because she felt hers getting warm. Just as she turned toward him, she saw Bill standing next to him. He grinned. "Red's my favorite, too."

"Well." She looked from Bill to Tyler. "That's nice. It's great to see you two." She gestured toward the urn on the table. "Like some coffee?"

"I'd rather have a soft drink if you have it," Bill said.

She directed him to another table. "In that white cooler. The guy behind the table is John. He can help you."

Tyler glanced at the retreating back of Bill, then back to Megan. "To be truthful, I've always favored the color blue." Tyler lifted his hands as if warding off an attack. "Not that I have anything against red, but that was a ploy to start a conversation."

"Since we're being honest," she said as seriously as she could manage without laughing, "I will admit I have nothing against blue either."

He laughed lightly, all the way from his full, wide lips over those white, white teeth, to his eyes that did not look blue-gray at all today but as clear, sky blue as the shirt he wore. At that moment, if she were asked if blue were her favorite color, she surely would reply, "It is now."

She returned his smile, and he reached for a cup and pressed the lever on the urn. After filling his cup, he stepped aside to pour creamer. "Others might be wanting coffee."

Megan looked around. Her friend Libby was talking to Bill, who turned up his soft drink can for a big swallow. Dan and Joan Adair, the middle-aged couple whose turn it was to greet visitors this Sunday, were talking with a man, woman, and two small children. Mrs. Potts, an older woman who came to greet visitors almost every Sunday, walked around, making sure everyone was being welcomed and had refreshments if they wanted them.

"We didn't have many visitors today," Megan told him. "But of course they don't always come back here. We just like to make it available. Last Sunday, being Easter, we had a lot of visitors."

Tyler took a sip of his coffee, then lowered the cup. "I'm not exactly a visitor. I'm a member here."

"Oh." Megan wanted to ask so many things, such as why he hadn't moved his membership when he was away for two years. Was he on a work project and knew he'd come back? Had he attended church while he was away? Had he been getting higher education but kept his membership in his home church as many college students did? Sipping her coffee she told herself this was not the time to ask such personal questions. Or was it?

Before she could decide, he spoke. "I take it you're not a visitor either."

She lowered her cup. "No. But I'm on the outreach committee of the singles' class, so when I've invited someone to church, I think I should be in here in case they come."

The mere flicker of his glance toward Bill was hardly noticeable but enough to tell her he knew she had invited Bill as well as him. For some strange reason she wanted to explain, as if it needed explanation. Of course it didn't. This wasn't a date where she had asked two guys to accompany her. And, too, she had asked them both to come to the singles' class, not the worship service. Tyler would know a Christian invites all the people he can to church so they can hear the gospel message preached.

Tyler drank his coffee, then walked over to the trash can and tossed in the cup. When he turned, the pastor walked in and went right up to Tyler and grasped his arm. "You know how to reach me, Tyler. Anytime."

Tyler nodded. "I know. Thanks. Good sermon."

A wistful kind of smile came over Tyler's face as he watched the pastor march over to the visiting family and begin talking.

"Tyler, some of us singles usually go out to eat together after church. You're welcome to join us."

"Thanks, but I'd be a wet blanket today. Not quite up to group socializing."

"Well, would you be up to a quiet lunch with a woman in red who has a good listening ear in case anyone wants to talk?"

Before he could answer, Bill and Libby walked up. Libby reached out to shake Tyler's hand. "I thought you looked familiar. You were a couple of years ahead of me in high school. Wow. Seems like decades ago."

"I believe it was," Tyler said with a grin.

"Ohh, I'm getting old," Libby said. "Anyway, in high school the girls always looked up to upperclassmen." She glanced at Bill. "Especially if they played football."

Bill's chest seemed to expand, and he smiled broadly.

"I married one," Libby said. "A football player, I mean. After going to college. Moved away for several years. I'm divorced now. Been back about a year. Anyway, nice to see you again."

"Thanks, Libby. Nice to see you."

Megan couldn't imagine why Libby went into such a long spiel about her personal life. Well, maybe she could. All sorts of situations existed with those in the singles' class, and they were honest about it for the most part. Megan was open about her own situation but didn't feel comfortable going into details.

She had the feeling Tyler was not one to be open about his personal life. Maybe that's what interested her so. She felt she knew Bill. He seemed like an all right person, but likely an open book. Tyler. . .intrigued her.

Bill spoke up. "Hey, Tyler. Libby said a bunch of people are going out to eat. Want to go with us?"

"Sorry. Not today. You guys have fun."

Bill touched Megan's arm. "Oh, the guys at the station loved the fruit." He laughed. "The candy, too."

Megan's gaze landed immediately on Tyler's face. A slow blink of his eyes and a slight nod indicated agreement that, yes, the fruit was good. She hadn't included candy in his basket.

Well, Megan, pat yourself on the back. You did a great job. You were out to prove to yourself that your feelings for Tyler were not personal. All right, you proved it—to Tyler, to Bill, and to anyone else who might be within hearing range. She felt it coming—the warmth that would color her cheeks.

Tyler's chest rose slightly, and he said, "I need to be going."

They said their good-byes and made a few expected comments she barely heard.

With a glance at them all he lifted his hand in farewell, and his tall frame, topped by that wonderful head of wheat-colored hair, headed for the doorway.

Megan wondered what his parting glance had revealed.

Likely the heat that had reached her cheeks.

Red was fast becoming her least favorite color.

ᕽᕽ

"Hey, Megan."

Megan looked over to see who called to her. Three young girls were gathered in the church parking lot. She immediately recognized Penny, who looked adorable with her blond curls touching her shoulders. Megan lifted her hand in greeting, and Penny called her over.

"Be right with you," Megan said to her friends. She walked over to the young people. Penny introduced her friends, Dru and Shauna, and said they were trying to decide where to eat lunch. Megan laughed, glancing at the singles' gathering a short distance away. "We have that problem, too. Tunnel Road is full of places to eat, but no one wants to make the decision."

The two other girls stepped aside and began a conversation of their own, when Penny reached out and touched Megan's arm. A concerned look came into her eyes. "I saw Tyler leaving in his car, but I didn't know he was coming to church today. Did he go to your class?"

Megan shook her head. "I think he only came to the worship service. But he did come into the fellowship hall for coffee afterward." Trying not to sound as if she were prying, she added, "I invited him to join us for lunch, but I guess he has other plans."

Penny shook her head. "I don't think so. He just needs a little push to get back into things. He's been gone two years. So. . ." She shrugged.

"Push" was the word that stuck in Megan's mind. She had the distinct feeling that Penny was suggesting she "push" Tyler into socializing. That reminded her of a saying, "A woman chases a man until he catches her." How to go about such a thing she didn't know—she warned herself not to go there.

Megan smiled. "You guys have fun."

"You, too."

She turned to Penny's friends. "Nice to meet you," she said.

Dru and Shauna responded in like manner; then the three of them stepped into Penny's car. Hurrying over to the singles, Megan wondered what Tyler was doing. He didn't appear antisocial in the fellowship hall. Come to think of it, he was more social with her than anyone else. But apparently he had other plans for lunch. Or simply didn't care to lunch with the singles. Or. . .her.

Warning herself not to second-guess Tyler, she turned her attention to the conversations going on as she walked up to the singles. Bill was telling Derek about a high school football game. Libby remembered the game and praised Bill's having made several touchdowns. Kay glanced heavenward as if high school football meant little to her. Megan grinned, then tried to act interested. She should be content that two people she invited to church came today, not concerned with why one didn't accept the invitation to lunch.

Bill insisted on driving his car since he was new to the

group and they were so nice to invite him.

Derek rode in front. Megan sat between Libby and Kay in back. After they decided on O'Henry's Restaurant in Asheville and Bill started the car, Megan thought it perfectly logical she should ask, "Bill, do you know Tyler very well?" since they had been in the fellowship hall together.

He turned off Montreat Road onto Highway 70. After a thoughtful moment he spoke. "Not really. He was ahead of me in school. Long time ago I heard something. I think his parents were killed by a drunk driver. I heard a few things, but since I didn't know him well, I don't really know." He shrugged.

Well, that didn't give her much information. But how terrible to lose one's parents that way. And Penny being so young.

"I heard stuff, too," Libby said. "But I don't know either."

Megan looked over at Libby, whose expression was as vague as her comment. "Over the years I was busy with an unfaithful husband who turned abusive, then the divorce and all. Not much time to think about what was going on with other people."

The silence intimated something, but Megan told herself she was imagining things. Just because no one was offering information about Tyler didn't mean they were holding something back.

Libby leaned forward and touched the back of Bill's seat. "So, Bill," she said, and flashed a smile as her gaze caught the rearview mirror, "did you play football in college, too? My ex played in high school. We married right out of high school." Her voice became an octave lower. "A mistake."

Bill apparently sensed the downward spiral the conversation was taking and, after a few more comments about football, began talking about his life as a policeman. He prefaced it with, "This is not a big crime area, but a few interesting things do occur."

He dominated the conversation with interesting tales about a cop's life as he made the turn and drove onto Interstate 40, heading for Asheville.

While Bill and Libby apparently enjoyed the conversation immensely, Megan thought Derek and Kay were tolerating it. Derek was a pleasant guy who had served in the military for several years and returned to find his fiancée had found another. Megan had gone out with him a couple of times. She could relate to his being-dumped experience, but they had never clicked beyond being friends—although not close ones.

Kay, who had grown up in the area but had gone away to school, had been back for about six months. Now she had her master's degree and taught at Asheville-Buncombe Technical College. She'd said very little about her personal life except that she'd gotten away from the Lord for a few years and had returned to Him and the area. She lived in a very nice condo located near her parents' home.

Megan was accustomed to Kay's being more a listener than a talker, contrary to Libby, and was surprised when Kay said, "I never was into football very much. My sport was track."

Derek turned to see Kay better. "Really? That was my sport."

They were all bonded by sports, Megan's being swimming. They were still talking about the possibility of going to the beach together during the summer when they arrived at O'Henry's.

When their orders came, they looked tasty. But their attention turned to the three people following a waitress down another aisle.

Bill spoke about the same time Megan saw them. "I guess that's why Tyler didn't come with us."

They agreed. He was with an elderly couple Megan recognized as being church members and former missionaries. *To Korea*, she thought.

Now was that sweet. . .or what?

five

"I am such a hypocrite," Penny muttered to her reflection in the mirror as she put the finishing touches to her makeup. She and Shauna were heading out to the first Christian student union meeting that evening since returning from spring break.

She had even been a hypocrite to Shauna. She'd seen Shauna around school. When they were on student council in high school together, they found out each planned to go to Western after they graduated. Penny wanted to stay nearby, needing to be close enough to visit Tyler whenever she could. Shauna said she couldn't afford to go out-of-state and was given the option of staying in a dorm or getting a car, and she chose the dorm. Western offered the nursing program they both wanted.

Penny had been the one to suggest they might ask to be roommates. She offered to give Shauna rides home on weekends and during breaks. As it turned out, the two became great friends and told each other everything—except the truth about Tyler. Penny's vagueness had led Shauna to believe Tyler was teaching, which he was, but to fellow inmates at the Craggy Correctional Center.

Although their friendship now was genuine, she knew her every move was based on guilt. She had no doubt God had forgiven her. She'd even begged Him over and over and cried and cried, while knowing that wasn't necessary. All one had to do was ask and be sincere, and God forgave. But she couldn't forgive herself for being such a coward and carrying around such a secret.

The only people with whom she'd talked about it were Beth and John Templeton, retired missionaries to Korea. They became her foster parents until her eighteenth birthday and asked her to call them Beth and John, or even address them as parents if she wished. Penny said she'd like to call them Granddad and Grandmom, since they were treating her like the grandparents she barely remembered.

They said she didn't have to talk about it if she didn't want to. But Penny hadn't wanted to drive a car for quite a while, so they took her to visit Tyler on weekends while she was in her senior year, then during the summer.

Finally, after seeing Tyler paler and thinner than she ever had, she broke down on the way back from a visit and told the Templetons she was the criminal, not Tyler, and they probably wouldn't want to keep her anymore.

"What I've done is not right, is it?" she had wailed. "I let my brother go to prison when I should be there."

Neither of the Templetons answered her question. Instead Beth began telling her own story. When just a child and in a missions class at church, she thought the most exciting thing in the world would be to go to some faraway country and feed poor children and help their sinful little hearts find Jesus. As she grew older she no longer mentioned it, and when it came to mind, she staunchly rejected such an idea. "I was running from God as much as Jonah was running from God when he sailed for Tarshish instead of Nineveh. The storm came up, and he was thrown overboard from the ship and swallowed by a big fish."

She made the analogy that the big fish that swallowed her was the world. She was running from God's calling for her life. Ultimately, after some episodes she felt too ashamed to talk about, she came back to the Lord because she was being eaten alive by the filth and muck of the wrong kind of living.

When Beth wiped a tear from her cheek, Penny knew Beth still felt sorry, although the Lord had forgiven her.

John interjected that he, too, had things in his life he was ashamed of, and even after the Lord saved him, he had to work hard on his weaknesses, like being patient.

They joked about John's having to be patient with Beth, who had an impulsive personality and often wanted to do things on the spur of the moment while John wanted to make plans.

In spite of her tears Penny had laughed along with them. At that time she told them everything about the night she was driving and had the accident and Tyler took her punishment.

"How did you ever get over feeling guilty?" Penny asked Beth.

"After I met John and told him everything," she said. "John said if God forgave me, then my sins were as if they had been dumped into the Dead Sea where nothing could exist. When God forgives, man has no right not to forgive." She had smiled. "Maybe your telling us tonight will help you forgive yourself."

Penny had nodded. Talking about it had helped. She knew God forgave her. But how could she not feel like a hypocrite while her brother was locked away in a prison when he'd done nothing to deserve that?

"How can I ever repay him?" she asked.

Both John and Beth shook their heads. "You can't," John said. "Just as we can't do enough to repay Jesus for dying on the cross for us."

After that, Penny began to call them Grandmom and Granddad, feeling closer to them than anyone else on earth besides her brother. She would find a way to repay Tyler.

Only then would her heart be free of guilt.

≥≥

"Don't you ever date?" Tyler asked when Penny came home from college for the weekend.

"Oh, Tyler." Her ponytail swung around with the shaking of her head. She acted as if he'd said something dreadful. "Finals are coming up. You, being a teacher, know how tough teachers are on their students. Dating is a luxury, and this is no time for luxuries."

"All work and no play, you know." Tyler shook his finger at her.

She huffed. "You're one to talk. Who are you dating?"

"Me?" He held up the wrench he was about to take into a bathroom to use on a pipe that was obviously stopped up. The sink had drained more and more slowly until the water barely seeped down. "Who do you think will do the odd jobs around here? Not to mention the cooking and the cleaning and the laundry—"

She laid down the pencil she was using to make notes from a book and stood. Her pretty face took on a crushed appearance. "I'll do those things, Tyler."

"Sit!" He spoke as if he were training a dog, which might have been easier. "I'm kidding with you, Penny. If anything, I don't have enough to do instead of too much." He didn't want to make her feel bad by saying he loved the freedom of going from room to room, having chores to do, cooking his own dinner, or just rocking on the front porch, enjoying the freedom and fresh air.

Reluctantly she sat.

"Now," he said, "as soon as I get that sink unplugged, I'm cooking spaghetti for supper. That suit you?"

She nodded. "I'll do the salad."

He started to walk from the kitchen, but her words stopped him. "Okay, big guy. If you were kidding, answer my question. Who are you dating?"

"That, my dear, is for me to know," he jested.

"Yeah, yeah. I know what that means." He chuckled, leaving the kitchen, but he heard her final words. "I could suggest somebody."

"I can't hear you," he called. "Now hit the books."

While working on the pipe, he had a good idea whom she would suggest. The beautiful red-haired woman who drove a red car and wore red clothes. Megan had passed by the house one evening when he was on the porch with an after-supper cup of coffee. They'd waved; then her car was followed by another. He figured she was showing the Campbells' house to a prospective buyer.

But dating was not something he could consider doing casually. He was no longer a young, impulsive guy, and having a prison record wouldn't sit well with respectable people. He wanted to settle into the town slowly, be accepted for who he was instead of having to answer personal questions because he'd just returned to the area. He would continue going to the worship service, then ease into that singles' class after he'd been around for a while.

The following day, on Saturday, he and Penny went to the garden shop and bought plants for the flower beds. "Only things like pansies that the frost won't kill," Penny warned. "Mom used to say that after Dad would say there could be frost even in May."

They laughed lightly together, remembering their mom and dad. After they died, Penny couldn't talk about them without sobbing. He was glad she now only wore a wistful expression. She glanced at him. "Grandmom said the same thing." She smiled. "It was good, living with them, Tyler."

He nodded. "I had lunch with them Sunday. They're good people. I'm grateful to them."

He didn't mention the Templetons said Penny was living with guilt. He knew it was true but didn't know what to do about it. Maybe more time would ease her pain. Each time he wondered if he'd done the right thing, taking her punishment and leaving her with guilt she couldn't shake, he came to the same conclusion. Yes, he'd do it again. She was proving to be a smart, responsible, loving young woman. If she'd gone to a juvenile center, there's no telling what she might have become. He couldn't imagine anyone who hadn't done things for which they had felt guilty. With time she'd be okay.

Returning home after their shopping trip, he pulled into the driveway and popped the trunk of Penny's car so they could take out the plants. After eating burgers they'd picked up at a fast-food place, they spent the afternoon bringing the beds to life with multicolored pansies. He loved working with Penny and getting his hands in the dirt and feeling the sunshine on his face.

He must have been in the basement getting tools when Megan drove up the mountain road. She was driving back down when Penny jumped up, waved vigorously, and motioned for Megan to stop.

Megan pulled into the driveway behind Penny's car. Tyler

was well aware Megan had not stopped on her own but because Penny waved her down. Would she have stopped otherwise? He couldn't very well ask.

He became well aware, too, of how grungy he looked in shorts and an old shirt smudged with dirt. She looked as gorgeous in her ivory-colored suit as she had in the navy blue and the red. The conversation was light, about general things such as the flowers, her showing the Campbell property to a client, Penny's school.

"And what are you doing these days, Tyler?" she asked, giving him a smile as dazzling as the sun that was turning her red hair to that golden sheen.

"Nothing special," he said. "I'm making some needed repairs in and around the house." He gestured toward the beds. "Planting flowers."

Penny punched him in the arm. "Tyler, you're teaching that class at the center."

"Oh, yes, that," he said.

Megan seemed interested. "What center?"

"The juvenile center for boys. I'm teaching there five mornings a week." He added quickly, "Including a Bible study."

"That sounds interesting. I'd love to hear more about that."

He nodded, looked down, and brushed at his hands, covered with dirt, then wiped them on his shorts.

After a brief pause Megan said, "Tyler, the singles are having a cookout at a local boys' camp in a couple of weeks. We'd love for you to come." She looked at Penny. "You, too, Penny, if you'd like."

"I'm studying for finals," Penny said. "But Tyler could probably come."

Tyler didn't commit himself. "Thanks, Megan." He felt his

head bobbing up and down, so he stopped it.

Soon Megan left. He refused to look when he heard her high heels clicking on the driveway, although he liked seeing her. That's because he'd been so long without female companionship, he told himself.

As soon as Megan's car disappeared down the road, Penny's hands were on her hips. "I can't believe you, Tyler."

He tried his innocent look. "What?"

"She did everything but come right out and ask you for a date."

"No way."

"Yes way! She said she'd lo—o—ove to hear more about your teaching, then invited you to a cookout."

He shrugged. "She's on the outreach committee, Penny. It's her job."

"The gleam in her eyes when she looks at you isn't her job."

"Penny, I'm not into the dating scene. I'm too old for that. I get to know people—then, who knows."

"I know," she retorted. "Let's talk about this later."

He didn't want to, but over dinner she brought it up again. "Tyler, I think we need to tell people the truth."

He stared. "The truth?"

She nodded. "I was seventeen when the accident happened. I was young and foolish and scared. But I can handle telling the truth now. You sacrificed two years for me. You don't need to suffer anymore. That's why you can't get back into things. Why you won't date anybody."

"No, Penny," he said adamantly. "To bring this out now would be like undoing what I did for the past two years. I did it because I love you and some juvenile center was not for you. You've proved your worth, Penny. That's what I wanted for you. We just need to go from here, not undo what is over and done. Please."

She nodded, but he hated knowing she still carried the guilt around like a bag of rocks, weighing her down.

He tried not to show regret when Penny said the situation was keeping him from pursuing a relationship with Megan. All he said was, "Penny, we're both tiptoeing through life right now."

six

On Sunday Megan's rising hope plummeted when Tyler came into the fellowship hall with Bill after the worship service. He said he'd just stopped in to say hi. Again he turned down her invitation to lunch. He talked to several people, greeted a visiting middle-aged couple, conversed with the pastor, then nodded at her before slipping out.

She had the same reaction as when she'd seen him the day before, working with Penny in the flower beds. His dark blond hair was intriguingly sun-streaked. She almost laughed aloud, remembering the dirt smeared across his forehead and his nose that looked as if it had a little too much sun. Today, however, his face and nose were simply tanned. She remembered his muscular arms and chest and how fit he looked.

She couldn't quite figure him out. She thought he liked her, but she supposed not enough to pursue a relationship—not that she was ready for one.

That's why it surprised her on Monday when the bell on the door of the real estate office jangled and, looking up from her desk, she saw Tyler. After a brief glance around, he walked straight toward her. He hesitated, seeing she was on the phone.

"I'll check on that," she said, "and return your call later. Thank you." She hung up, grateful the client on the other end of the line wasn't long-winded. She felt warmth rising to her cheeks for no reason whatsoever except surprise that he'd come into the office. "And what can I do for you, sir? List your house? Help you find a second one?"

"Nothing quite so grand," he said. "This isn't a business call." She heard the nervousness in his laugh as he glanced over at the man staring at him from the other desk. The man nodded, and Tyler did the same, then looked again at Megan. "I know this is short notice, but since I was in the neighborhood, I thought I'd stop in and see if you'd like to have lunch with me."

Megan could hardly believe it. She'd given up on him. Now that was a silly thought. There had been nothing to give up on. Nothing had even started. But now he was asking her to lunch? She glanced at the wall clock, then at Ted, her boss, who kept looking at the computer on his desk but was playing with the tip of his nose as he had the habit of doing. Ted owned the business, but lunchtime was up to her, whenever she could manage it. "I could go in about thirty minutes," she said tentatively.

"Great," Tyler said. "I'll take a stroll around town and come back at noon."

By that time Ted had walked over and stuck out his hand. "Ted Bray. Are you new in town?"

"Yes and no," Tyler responded. "I'm Tyler Corbin. My parents lived here for many years, and I've just returned."

"Corbin. I've heard the name. Well, nice having you back, Tyler. If we can help you out in any way, just let us know."

"Not looking for a house right now," Tyler said. "Thanks."

As soon as the bell jangled and the glass door closed behind Tyler, Ted turned and leaned his hands on the edge of Megan's desk. "Sounds like you're getting back in circulation."

Megan didn't like the way he had of insinuating he had the right to know about her personal life. He had asked her out a couple of weeks after she started working for him, but she told him she didn't care to go out with anyone. She was getting over a difficult relationship.

"Circulation?" Megan tried to laugh it off. "We're not going on a date, Ted. He asked me to lunch. I've been trying to get him into the singles' class at church. He only goes to the worship service. Seems I've invited you more than a few times."

"Right, but you turned me down for lunch."

"Well, you haven't shown any interest in church. He did."

Ted straightened. "You mean if I go to church, you'll go to lunch with me?"

She shook her head. How did she get herself into such verbal messes? "No, I don't make those kinds of deals."

"Mmm. I see." He started walking back toward his desk, playing with the tip of his nose. Before sitting in his chair, he looked at the ceiling and mumbled, "Corbin? Hmm."

Megan knew Ted's remarks and actions had a hint of jealousy. He was nice enough in his way. He had said he'd experienced a difficult divorce, got to see his two children not nearly often enough, but he wasn't a Christian. She'd been disappointed in her boyfriend who had been a Christian. She certainly didn't want to get mixed up with one who wasn't. Life was difficult enough without that, she'd learned. What she wanted was someone who shared her beliefs and was a born-again Christian, active in service to others.

She'd already thought Tyler had those attributes, but she didn't know him well. She wanted to get away from the office and Ted's lifting of his eyebrows and glancing at her occasionally. She left before noon and was relieved to see Tyler strolling down the sidewalk toward her.

He let her choose where to go, and she chose her favorite lunch place, the Veranda. The food was wonderful, and Jeff, the proprietor, always made her feel welcome.

"Inside or out?" the waitress asked.

Megan looked at Tyler. "Outside okay?" he asked.

"Perfect," she said.

The day was perfect, too. Warm with the usual light breeze. They sat at a table covered with a red-and-white-checkered tablecloth and fresh flowers in the center.

"Beautiful flowers," Tyler said.

Megan followed his gaze to the flower boxes along the banister. Trumpet vines traveled along the stairwell railing. Two stories below were well-kept flower beds, profuse with colorful pansies much like what Tyler and Penny had planted. She smiled at him. "They are beautiful." She could appreciate a man who liked flowers—and admitted it.

They both chose flavored tea. Today's flavor was mango. She chose a half tuna salad with lettuce and tomato on a croissant and a cup of Hungarian mushroom soup.

Jeff came out and shook hands with Tyler as Megan introduced them. After some deliberation Tyler decided on potato soup and the BST, which Jeff had described as bacon, spinach, and tomato on John Durst bread—a special blend of a tasty South Carolina recipe.

While they ate, Megan asked questions, and Tyler talked about the days when he'd lived in the area and had taught fifth grade. Megan found Tyler to be charming, witty, intelligent, and interesting. But he skirted some subjects such as when she asked if he'd gone away for higher education.

He seemed to hedge a moment before saying, "Let's say it was a kind of sabbatical." He began talking about teaching at the juvenile center. She felt he really liked that and cared about the boys. .

"Do you think you'll go back to teaching public school?" she asked as they shared a piece of Italian cream cake.

"I want to be outside for a while before trying to return to an inside job, enclosed by four walls." She wasn't sure if he was serious when he said, "I might even consider real estate."

His warm look and his smile made her heart skip a beat.

20

"Don't even try to come home in this driving rain, Penny," Tyler warned. "You probably need to study anyway."

Penny admitted that was true, but she sounded as if the rain had dampened her spirits. Maybe he could lift them. "Besides," he said, "you might cramp my style." He paused, then added, "Since I'm dating now."

"Dating!" He held the phone away from his ear and her scream. "Who? Her? I mean, Megan?"

He laughed. Yes, she sounded much better even if she had burst his eardrum. He had told himself he would give the semblance of having a life of his own so Penny would get over her guilt and enjoy the fun of being a young college girl.

"Well," he said. "It was lunch. But that's a start."

"Oh, Tyler. Give me the details."

He did and didn't feel he was embellishing the event at all. He felt the excitement he heard in his own voice. At the same time he warned himself not to take one lunch too seriously. Megan could have been thinking he was a prospective client, maybe wanting to sell the big brick house and find something smaller. Also he knew firsthand a woman would not take his prison term lightly. He needed to guard his heart.

"I will stay here, Tyler. Are you seeing her this weekend?"

"I expect so," he replied, thinking he'd likely see her at church. But he had to take any relationship slowly. "Now you study and keep up those good grades. I love you, Penny."

"Love you, too, Tyler. Oh, so much."

"Bye-bye," he said quickly, knowing her "Oh, so much" meant she was again thinking of the past, not the present. Maybe someday she could go on without the past hovering like those black clouds overhead.

April showers bombarded the little town for days, and the news reporters warned of flooding in Buncombe and nearby counties, and rock slides down Interstate 40, near the Tennessee border.

This reminded him of the floods that came two years ago. The only thing that kept his picture and the write-up about his arrest and incarceration off the front page of the *Black Mountain News* was the flood that took precedence, caused by the hurricane that drenched Florida and reached as far as the mountains of western North Carolina. The entire area had to be evacuated. A couple of lines of his story appeared near the back in the Asheville paper. He'd often thanked God that his picture and story hadn't been splattered over the front page of the newspaper.

On Sunday, his third visit to the church, he still didn't attend the singles' class but went to worship service and afterward talked to the Templetons about some repairs they mentioned needing to have done at their house.

"We didn't mean for you to do them," John Templeton said, when Tyler showed up on their doorstep on Monday after teaching his morning classes at the juvenile center.

"I want to, if you trust me to do it."

Beth appeared at John's side. "Let him in before he drowns, John."

While doing a few minor chores, the aroma of chocolate chip cookies wafted through the house. As soon as Beth took them from the oven, she insisted he and John sit at the table to have cookies and a cup of coffee.

He'd invited them out to lunch a few weeks ago to express his appreciation for taking care of Penny. They'd said she was more of a blessing to them than they could ever be to her.

Now Beth surprised him. "The restaurant wasn't the place to tell you, Tyler. But Penny told us she was responsible for the accident, not you. I don't think she's told anyone else."

"We admire you so much," John said. "I don't know many people who would do that. Even the best of persons might say she should take her own punishment."

Tyler set his cup down and looked from one to the other. "After our parents died and I became her legal guardian, I felt I failed her. That was the least I could do to make up for it."

"You didn't fail her, Tyler," Beth said. "She talked to us. She knew right from wrong and made some bad choices. She can't seem to forgive herself."

He knew that, but none of them knew what to do about it. "Maybe time will help."

During the following weeks he worked at the Templetons, and after the sun appeared again, he repaired the leak around their chimney.

seven

Megan had been on the phone and the computer for about thirty minutes talking with a man named Ed Heffron, who asked more questions about her than he did about his possible listing. He wouldn't be home until late for her to see his house. She didn't feel right about it and said so to Ted.

Ted stretched, then stared at her for a while. Finally he spoke. "I could use a break here. What about our getting a bite of lunch and talking this over? Maybe I could go with you for the listing."

The going-to-lunch part was too much like a date. If she went with him once, she'd be open to do it again. And, too, she wanted to keep her lunch hour open in case Tyler stopped by. She hoped she wasn't wrong in thinking they had gotten along fabulously.

"Ted, when you hired me, you said I'd have to hold my own like the male Realtors. So I think I'd better handle this myself in my own way."

Ted's sneer indicated his offer had not been business at all, but personal. A slight grin touched his lips, and he peered at her. "Instead of worrying about this man who wants you to see his house at night, you'd be wise to check out that Corbin guy if that's where your interests lie."

Check him out? "What does that mean?"

He shrugged, but the smug look remained. "Just giving you a little friendly advice. I've heard some talk, and there's a lot of speculation." He lifted his hands. "That's all I'm saying."

Megan didn't like the sound of that. It could be jealousy on Ted's part since he was lonely and interested in her. But she had heard vague comments from other acquaintances about Tyler, most speculating about where he'd been for two years. Of course that didn't mean anything was wrong. All she'd seen from him was admirable. So he left a teaching position. She'd left her position in Charlotte to come and live with Aunt Eva. People did that. She didn't like the suspicions Ted put in her mind. She had no reason for suspicion. Just because her fiancé had been untrustworthy didn't mean she had to check out every other man she might be interested in as if he were a criminal or something.

Okay, these were modern times. Tyler had asked her to lunch. There was no reason whatsoever she couldn't ask him. . . something. Not in front of Ted, though. "I'm going home to eat with Aunt Eva today," she told Ted.

Aunt Eva was pleased to see her and said she'd fix them both a lunch. Megan went to her room, found a phone book, then dialed Tyler's home number. She wasn't sure what time he finished teaching at the center, but he answered on the third ring.

He sounded genuinely glad to hear from her.

"Tyler, you mentioned you might be interested in going into real estate. Maybe you'd like to go with me tonight to see a house for possible listing."

"That would be a pleasure. Thanks, Megan. May I pick you up?"

She told him where Aunt Eva lived, and he knew the area.

She hung up and took a deep breath. *"A pleasure,"* he'd said.

Business and personal wouldn't work with Ted. Maybe it could with Tyler.

That thought was reinforced when Tyler picked her up in his luxury car. He looked quite professional wearing dress slacks, white shirt, and tie. The spring evening was much too warm for a suit coat.

Megan wore one of her short-sleeved tailored suits, her favorite attire for business. She had been pleased when Tyler asked if he could drive them to the appointment. Although she liked being independent, she had to admit it felt good just sitting back enjoying the view and experiencing easy camaraderie with this man.

They laughed about his stories of sledding down a hill on the golf course after a heavy snow. "Those were the days of many mishaps," he said. "That tree right over there had a way of jumping out in front of me every time."

Fortunately the hill was a slope instead of a high one on which children would pick up great speed.

When Mr. Heffron answered the doorbell and greeted them kindly, she realized he was a grandfatherly type and she would have been comfortable seeing him alone.

Megan introduced herself and Tyler.

"Call me Ed," the man said. He looked at Tyler thoughtfully. "I sold life insurance to a couple named Corbin. They were my clients for many years." He said their first names, and Tyler confirmed they were his parents.

Ed mentioned having found them to be a fine couple. He then returned to the business at hand. "I've been in Greensboro for several days," he said. "There's a condo near my son that interests me. This house is too big for me anymore, and the upkeep on the yard is more than I want."

They walked around the outside, and Megan made notes as they talked about the size of the lot, square footage of the house, age of the roof, and any repairs that needed to be made. If he listed the property, she could have a surveyor confirm the statistics and a photographer take pictures.

Ed took them inside, and they looked at each room. When they returned to the kitchen, the man looked around thoughtfully. "This has been my home for so long, it's hard for me to think of leaving it," he said. "But I think it's probably time, now that I'm retired and live alone."

Tyler and Ed spoke about the loss of their loved ones, and Tyler mentioned he'd wondered what to do with the big brick house he lived in alone except when Penny came home from college.

The men talked of repairs, and Ed asked Tyler his opinion on several things. Tyler responded that if he were to buy the house, he'd want that broken back step fixed and the water-stained ceiling tile in the family room replaced or painted.

Megan felt the three of them related well. She quoted an asking price and said what she thought it would sell for. Ed was pleased since the house had been paid off a few years before and he'd have enough from the sale to buy a nice condo.

"I was sure he would sign a listing contract," Megan said after she and Tyler left Ed's house and got in the car.

Tyler agreed, turning the key in the ignition. "He seemed to be pleased with all the suggestions." After backing out into the street and driving alongside the golf course, he added thoughtfully, "He may just want to think about it further. As he said, it's not easy leaving a family home." His tone of voice lowered slightly. "I know."

"It wasn't too hard for my dad," she said before thinking.

A feeling of chagrin washed over her. "Oh, I think I sounded bitter."

"Tell me about it," he said.

Megan realized she wanted to tell him. "My dad left the family when I was a young child. My mother said he preferred another woman to his own wife and children." She could still feel the hurt. "That didn't do much for my self-esteem."

"You appear confident," Tyler said.

"I've learned," she said, "to put my faith in God instead of people. Too many have disappointed me."

Seeing his brow furrow and his lips seem to tighten, she decided to lighten the mood by changing the subject. "How are your classes going at the juvenile center?"

His face brightened immediately. "It's a real challenge. Much more than when I taught fifth grade. I loved that, but the boys at JC need me—or someone—to tell them about the Lord and help them see they can start over and make something of their lives."

"I think what you're doing is so admirable, Tyler," she said. "It takes a special kind of person to do it."

He shook his head. "I don't know about that."

She wasn't sure how to ask the questions in her mind. If he loved teaching fifth grade, why had he left town? For further study? Was he a rover who couldn't stay settled?

Before she even knew what to ask, she noticed darkness had fallen, and he pulled into the driveway at her aunt Eva's house. Aunt Eva would be embarrassed to be caught in her robe, so rather than chance that, Megan didn't ask Tyler if he'd like to go inside. Besides, they both had work in the morning.

He exited the car and walked around to hold on to the door she'd already opened. She liked his gentlemanly ways.

"Thanks for asking me to go with you, Megan." He closed the car door and leaned back against it. "I enjoyed seeing you at work. You make a great Realtor."

"That's nice to hear," she said. "I do appreciate your going with me."

"Anytime," he said and smiled.

She was aware of the coolness of the late evening, the relative quiet with only an occasional car passing, lights appearing in windows, insects beginning their night songs. She liked being with Tyler.

He remained leaning against the car. Was he reluctant to leave or just waiting for her to go inside?

"By the way," she said, "remember that singles' cookout I mentioned?"

He nodded.

"If you can go, would you like to come early and help?"

"I'll. . .think about it."

"Do you know how to get there? It's Camp Rocky Mount."

"I know it well," he said. "In fact I was a counselor there during my college years. Being a group leader was fun, but what I enjoyed most was taking those kids for hikes on trails I'd been running practically all my life."

Megan smiled. The more she knew of Tyler, the more she liked him. Yet she often had the impression he was holding something back. Or maybe she was too eager to know all about him.

She didn't mean to be pushy. "Please know you're welcome to come to the cookout, and you don't need to help. I just thought you might like to."

"We'll see." He stood straighter.

"Good night, Tyler."

"Good night, Megan." He reached out and took her hand for a moment, and she felt the gentle pressure of his fingers on hers. "Thanks again," he said quickly and let go.

She hurried to the door that was unlocked and opened it. About the same time she closed the door, she heard the sound of the car door closing.

Well, what had she expected? That he would walk up onto the porch with her and kiss her good night? That would be foolish. There were only a few steps from the driveway to the porch, and kissing good night on the porch would put them in plain view of the whole neighborhood. And it wasn't as if this had been a date. He hadn't asked her out. She had asked him to accompany her to a business appointment.

But his holding her hand was not a handshake by any means. She could still feel the gentle pressure. She let her fingers rest for a moment on her warm cheek.

eight

Late Friday afternoon Tyler headed out to the boys' camp for the cookout. When he reached the fork where one could go right or left, he took the left fork. A right turn led to the watershed and a dead end. Life was like that. One wrong decision and a person ended up where he hadn't really intended to go, and with a life changed forever.

He thought of Penny and how she'd changed after the accident. She'd become intent on being the best at whatever she tackled, academically and spiritually. He was proud of her. He only wished her efforts were completely motivated by the Lord and her own desires, and without traces of guilt.

He rolled down the car window as he drove along the road bordered by pines on each side, their branches making a shady canopy while the sun tried to make diamond-shaped brilliance where the rays peeked through. The aroma of fresh pine was clean and crisp. After turning into the camp and parking alongside other cars, he walked up the road, past the tennis courts, the dining hall, and bunkhouses. His counselor experience had sealed his commitment to teach lower grades so he could have an influence before the children ended up in a place like the juvenile center.

Nearing the crowd ahead, he thought of how he'd hedged with Megan when she'd asked him to the cookout. He wanted to get back into the mainstream of things with others his age. Maybe the cookout would be a good time to do that.

But for Megan's sake he didn't want to give others the impression he and Megan were too close until she knew him better. He was walking a line between letting her know him and not revealing too much. In a time like this he wished he were wiser.

As soon as he walked up he was greeted cordially and welcomed. Bill Probe came over and shook his hand. "Glad you could make it, Ty," he said, as if they were buddies. Tyler wondered if Bill's longer-than-necessary gaze was meant as some kind of warning. Did Bill know about his prison term? Were cops sworn to confidentiality like psychiatrists and priests?

Glancing around, he saw Megan about the time she saw him. Standing with her and another young man was Ted, Megan's boss. The three walked toward him. He felt a jolt at how beautiful she looked. He'd only seen her in tailored business suits. Now she wore jeans and a white button-down shirt, with the sleeves rolled up to her elbows. A thin, silver chain with a small heart hung around her neck. Little silver earrings sparkled in the sun when she moved her head. Her hair seemed more casual, in slight disarray, falling softly along her cheeks.

At a loss as to what to say other than she was gorgeous, he thought of saying she wasn't wearing red. His glance fell to her flip-flops, and he noticed her brightly polished toenails. "Still wearing red, I see," he said. Her gaze followed his, and they laughed together.

Then he remembered the two men were standing there. "You've met Ted," Megan said, and Tyler shook his hand. "Have you met Derek?" Tyler hadn't, although he'd seen him at church.

Megan turned to Derek. "Derek, would you like to introduce Ted around? I'll take Tyler. You, too, Bill?"

Bill declined. "I'm planning to stand near those hamburgers and be the first in line. I'm starving."

As they walked away, Megan linked her arm through Tyler's and spoke softly. "I think what he's hungry for is Libby. She's turning the burgers."

Tyler glanced over, and Libby waved a spatula at them. He waved back. Megan's arm tucked through his felt natural, as if it belonged there. It made him want to take her in his arms and hold her and tell her he hadn't expected to feel so strongly about anyone again. But they came to an older couple looking into the lake and talking about something there, probably minnows.

"Most of our group is young," Megan said. "But we like the fellowship of having a few older singles join us." He missed the warmth when she moved her arm away. "Mary, Fred."

They turned. They both looked to be in their late fifties or early sixties, about the age his parents would have been. Megan introduced them, adding that Fred had been a missionary for several years.

"Well, of course I know Tyler." Mary touched his arm. "At least I knew your parents. I was so sorry about what happened." She grimaced. "I lost my husband not long after that. He was sick for a long time." She took a deep breath. "Anyway, Fred lost his wife to cancer, too. We. . .understand each other."

Tyler nodded.

Fred spoke up then. "I knew your parents, too. You did a good thing, taking care of your sister like you did."

"Thank you," Tyler said, and wondered how much more

Fred and Mary knew. Their eyes held only friendliness and understanding.

"You took care of Penny after your parents died?" Megan asked when they walked away.

"I had custody. But I didn't do such a good job." He took a deep breath of the fresh air he hoped would clear away the unpleasant thoughts.

Megan stopped. "Why do you say that, Tyler? She seems like a wonderful girl."

His level gaze met hers. "Indeed she is. But I can't take the credit."

Any words Megan might have said were halted as they came upon several others sitting in folding lawn chairs farther along the lake.

Before long a bell was rung, Fred said a blessing, and then a line formed of about twenty-five or thirty people. "We don't have this many in our class," Megan told him. "Some brought friends." Each took a paper plate and went through the line, choosing burgers or hot dogs or both and all the trimmings, plus baked beans and assorted cookies.

Megan led him to a table where Bill sat with Libby, Derek, and Kay. Tyler put his plate across from the seat Megan had chosen. "I'll get drinks," he offered. "What would you like?" Walking toward the drink table, he realized he didn't know most of these singles, nor did they know him. Most guys his age would have moved away or be married with children.

When Tyler returned with their drinks, Ted was sitting next to Megan and Kay sat next to Ted.

"How's it going at the juvie center, Ty?" Bill asked.

Tyler felt as if everyone were looking his way, waiting for an answer. He told how the boys were receptive to his teaching, especially in his Bible class, and how he believed he could make a difference in most of their lives. "The boys are eager to share their stories," he said, "and most are victims of parents who didn't care or had never had any religious upbringing."

"That kind of background can be so devastating," Kay said, and they all agreed.

He glanced toward her, and from her expression, it seemed she wasn't making a simple statement but had seen the results of such firsthand.

"Yeah," Bill said after a big gulp of soda. "We can just about pick out where the troublemakers are going to come from. 'Course, it's a lot different now that kids from all backgrounds are getting into drugs."

Tyler almost held his breath. Especially when Ted said, "Tyler." He braced himself for what might come.

"Megan says you might be interested in real estate. That right?"

From there the conversations were light.

"Testing, testing," came a voice over a P.A. system. Megan said Fred had been asked to give a short devotional. His talk reminded Tyler of experiences he'd heard John Templeton mention in years past. Fred quoted the scripture about going "to the ends of the earth" with the gospel message beginning "in Jerusalem," which meant missionaries were needed in one's own backyard, so to speak.

After Fred's prayer, people began getting up from their tables. Bill offered to take everyone's plates and dump them. Derek jumped up to help. Ted was speaking in low tones to Kay.

"I'll have to stay and make sure everything is cleaned up," Megan said.

"Since I didn't come early to help," Tyler said, "maybe you'd let me stay late and help clean up."

"I'd like that," she said. "I've assigned certain chores to my cleanup crew, but you could make sure all the picnic tables are clear and wipe them." She told him where to get a pail, water, and a cloth.

He could tell she was a good leader, having delegated authority quite well. By the time the sun had faded and the sky was deepening, everything was cleaned up. Only a few of her friends remained to see if there was anything else.

There wasn't, and they said their good-byes.

"I see a Styrofoam cup over there by the trees," Tyler said, before he went to retrieve it.

After he deposited it in the trash can, he and Megan walked to the parking area where her car was parked near a grove of trees. When they reached it, she leaned against the side.

He heard the sincerity in her voice when she said softly, "I'm glad you came to the cookout, Tyler." He wondered if something personal might be in that remark. He hoped so.

He shoved his hands into his pockets. "I'll bet you say that to all the guys."

She gave him a sideways look. "You mean like Ted?"

He shrugged as if it didn't matter. "And Bill."

Her tone was saucy. "Yes, I certainly did."

"Hmm," he said, taking his hands out of his pockets to gesture with his palms up. "It's your job to invite singles to your class and your outings."

"Not my job. My mission." She lifted her chin. "Anyway, if you noticed, I gave only you my undivided attention."

He took a step closer. "Seems I remember your asking Bill to join us."

"Only to be polite. I knew he wouldn't go." Her eyes sparkled. "I hope that means you're jealous."

"Yes, I wouldn't want either of them to get close enough to step on your pretty red toenails."

The light banter became more serious when the smile left her face and she looked up at him and said, "I wouldn't let them."

Would she let him?

He shouldn't. But they were alone. Her lips parted slightly, as if she were waiting.

At the moment he felt as if they were the only two people in the world. Taking hold of her arms he leaned close, and she lifted her face to his. His arms circled her, and hers went around his neck. For one moment he tasted her sweet, warm lips against his own. Feeling her closeness, he cautioned. . . enough. He'd been a man in a desert, longing for water. Drinking too much would mean he'd surely drown.

Reluctantly he stepped back. Megan's hand rested against his chest for a moment. She smiled and hardly met his gaze. Then she reached for his hand and spoke quietly, as if she, too, wanted to hold on to that special moment. "I should go."

Tyler agreed. He saw the sky had darkened more. He loved the way she looked with the moonlight lying softly on her lovely face and hair. She hadn't let go of his hand, and she looked up at him. "I would love for you to meet my aunt Eva. Maybe next Sunday after church?"

"I have other plans."

The way she seemed to hold her breath and look disappointed was touching. She let go of his hand then.

He laughed lightly. "And my plans include you. Penny is finishing her first year of college. I want to take her out to eat. I'd love for you and your aunt Eva to join us." As much as he'd like for the two of them to be alone and get to know each other better, he felt this was the way to take things slowly. "John and Beth Templeton are planning to eat with us. You may know them from church."

She nodded. "Yes, I know of them. I would love to help celebrate the end of Penny's first year. If Aunt Eva is up to it, she would, too."

"Good. I'll make reservations at the Bistro at Biltmore. This needs to be special for Penny."

"She seems like such a wonderful girl," Megan said.

She's not the only one, Tyler thought later, as he followed Megan's car out of the parking area.

❦

"Oh, you shouldn't have," Penny said to Beth and John Templeton as she took the present that was wrapped in shiny white paper and tied with pink ribbon.

"Okay, take it back," Tyler said to the Templetons.

They all laughed when Beth chided, "Tyler Corbin, shame on you." While they waited for their dinner at the Bistro, Penny opened the gift—a prayer journal.

"Thank you so much. My other one is almost full." Looking at the Templetons' smiles and warmth in their eyes reminded her anew that they were like parents or grandparents to her.

Megan, sitting on the other side of Tyler at the round table, passed a card to her. "A little something from me," she said. Penny read the congratulatory sentiments aloud, then held up the gift card. She turned to Megan. "This is from my favorite place to shop for clothes. We must have the same taste."

"Well," Megan hedged. "In my line of work, I'm more

into tailored outfits right now." She looked at Tyler, and they smiled at each other.

"Oh, I see." Penny said, knowing Megan had asked Tyler what she'd like. "I really appreciate this."

"And what you always ask for," Tyler said, handing her a card. It was a funny one and contained what she never had too much of—cash.

She appreciated her gifts, but Penny knew those gifts were not the most important ones. "I love the presents," she said. "But more than that, I love each of you. Having you in my life and your being here with me tonight means the world to me."

Megan looked past Tyler and smiled sweetly at her. Tyler and the Templetons expressed how proud they were of her. When she felt her eyes tear up, Tyler said, "Now none of that. This is supposed to be a fun evening."

"These are tears of joy, Tyler." She tried blinking the moisture away. "Don't you know anything?"

"No," he said as if serious. "Only young college freshmen know everything."

She swiped at his arm, and they all laughed.

Penny was grateful for the laughter which lightened the mood that was welling up in her. She was grateful the waiter chose that moment to bring their food. The elegant presentation and wonderful aroma of their entrées—New York strip steak for Tyler, filet mignon for Penny and Megan each, toasted almond-topped mountain trout for John, and stuffed chicken breast for Beth—tantalized the senses.

After John said a prayer, they started eating their entrées. When John and Beth exchanged bites, Tyler cut a small piece and insisted Megan sample his and give him a bite of hers.

"We both have steak, Tyler," she reminded him.

"No matter," he said. "This has always been a ritual in our family. Everybody has to try what others are eating. It's a normal thing to do."

They were all laughing, trying to be discrete in such a nice place, but enjoyed tasting each other's food. During the rest of the evening Penny felt as if others watching them would think they were just a group of average, normal people engaged in light conversation.

But she wasn't average and normal. No matter how much fun she had or how much others accepted her, she had this nagging feeling she had to prove not just to Tyler and the Templetons, who knew the truth about her, but to herself and God that she was a worthy person.

Of course she knew God had forgiven her. But the more aware she became of His presence and His great love and forgiveness, the worse she felt. The Templetons had told her she should forgive herself. So had Tyler. She wanted to admit openly what happened; but, as Tyler said, his two years in prison would then be in vain.

Seeing Tyler with Megan helped some. Penny could tell Megan and Tyler liked each other in a special way. She had noticed how dark his eyes had become after Clare had abandoned him. Now she saw new life in him and a spark of light in his eyes again.

After dinner Tyler dropped off the Templetons, then drove Megan home. During the drive, Penny felt those mixed emotions again. She wanted Tyler to have someone special in his life. But if he and Megan became serious about each other, then he'd have to tell Megan the truth. Megan would then know Penny was not the smart, successful young person she appeared to be. Megan liked her, she could tell. But that would change. If she fell in love with Tyler, how would she feel about Penny's being responsible for his ruined reputation? So far as she knew, no one had said anything against Tyler. But gnawing at her was the fear that would happen. Many people had to be aware of it.

Later in bed Penny stared at the ceiling, thinking about her future. She knew she wanted a man who had a strong faith in God and put Him first in his life. But would that kind of man want her when he knew the truth about her past?

She had to turn the lamp back on and read from her Bible to get rid of that kind of thinking; otherwise she'd be awake all night. She fell asleep praying for everyone she knew and thanking God for how graciously He had blessed her.

❧

The next afternoon when she went to work, Penny took a book with her. Working as a desk clerk at the conference center where she checked people in afforded her a good bit of free time to think or read. Her thoughts that day reverted to two years ago when she'd worked in the snack shop where she'd met Rudy. She hadn't expected to encounter someone who would turn out to be so deceptive in a place where Christians came for retreats.

Nor had she thought she'd ever do what she did after being raised in a Christian home and taking Jesus Christ into her life as her Lord and Savior.

She was thinking of those things when she drove home that night after getting off at 11:00. She had just passed the conference grounds, when she glanced in the rearview mirror. She froze for a moment. A streetlight illuminated the face of the driver behind her. Then the car turned left, and she was alone on the lonely road.

That couldn't be. He wouldn't return to this area.

"Please, God," she prayed in a whisper. "Don't let that be Rudy."

nine

"What's this about Tyler?" Ted asked as soon as Megan came into the office on Monday morning.

She'd been on guard for anything Ted might say since the first time he had hinted they might go out together. She understood a man might react to having been turned down. But she didn't expect this. He must have seen her and Tyler walking together at the picnic. She had invited him to the picnic but had made it clear this was not a date.

Megan turned from him and walked around her desk, telling herself to remain calm and think for a moment before speaking. She set her briefcase on the desk, sat in her chair, opened the bottom drawer, and put her purse inside. She tucked her hair behind her ear, then reminded herself that was a nervous gesture. Finally she looked over at Ted and tried to smile sweetly. "Ted, whatever I do in my personal time is my business."

When he locked gazes with her and lifted his hand to the tip of his nose, she thought he got the message. He couldn't fire her for saying that. She faced her computer and turned it on. She refused to look at him but knew he rose from his chair and walked to her desk.

When he rested his hands on the edge opposite her she finally looked up. Okay, if he wanted to fire her, fine. Why couldn't her boss have been sixty years old and happily married? She braced herself for whatever he might say.

"You're right," he said. "But what happens with my business is my business."

She met his gaze. "And this has something to do with Tyler?"

"It absolutely does." He straightened and gazed down at her with a look of triumph. "I ran into Ed Heffron on Saturday at the hardware store. He wanted to know if Tyler Corbin worked for me."

For a moment she was at a loss for words, with Ted staring down at her as if he'd won some kind of contest in which the two of them had competed. "Ted, I decided it might not be wise to go to Mr. Heffron's place alone. I asked Tyler to go with me." She didn't like this defensive feeling. "We in no way indicated he is working for you. Is something wrong with his having gone with me?"

"Yes." Ted was nodding. "After I assured Heffron that Corbin doesn't work for me, he said okay, he'd probably list with us. He wondered if some of the rumors he'd heard were true."

"Rumors? About me and Tyler?" She couldn't control the high octave screech in her voice. Was Ted making this up?

He shook his head. "So far your reputation hasn't been besmirched. But that's not the first time I've heard vague comments about Tyler. Like I said before, for your own good, maybe you should check him out."

She knew the damage gossip or rumors could have. She didn't like asking the question she was about to ask, not of Ted anyway. But she did. "What have you heard, Ted?"

He shrugged and had a satisfied expression on his face. "I believe that comes under the definition of your, um. . .your personal business."

With that, he turned and strode back to his desk and began to concentrate on his computer screen—or at least pretended. She would love to have wiped that smug smile off his face.

Megan had difficulty concentrating on anything for the rest of the day. She called Ed Heffron, and he said he would come into the office midmorning and sign the papers. After he did, she tried to sound professional when she showed the signed contract to Ted. "I don't think your business has gone under yet."

His eyebrows shot up. "No, but it was a close one."

She wanted to get back to a friendly basis. "My daddy always told me close ones only count in horseshoes."

Ignoring her comment, he glanced at the contract and nodded. "Good job," he said.

"Thanks."

That was the trouble with working for a single man about the same age. Being only friends wasn't easy. But Ted did have some nice ways. He just wasn't for her. She tried to dismiss his remarks as jealousy, but she didn't think he was vindictive enough to make up things about Tyler. And if there was something, maybe he was doing right in bringing it to her attention. Obviously he wasn't repeating whatever Mr. Heffron had said. She couldn't be sure if Ted was toying with her or refraining from gossip.

The awful thing was, it had its effect. She could understand Ted was concerned that anyone would get the impression Tyler worked for him when he didn't.

Recalling their visit, she could understand why Mr. Heffron might think that, although she had been the one to do all the talking about the business side of things such as the possible selling price. Tyler had pointed out several things Mr. Heffron might want to repair before putting it on the market. He should paint the water-spattered wall above the kitchen sink and fix the broken step at the back porch. Tyler had suggested a cracked ceiling tile in the family room be replaced.

Now that she thought about it, she realized it might have been better if Ted had gone with her instead of Tyler. Tyler's presence would indicate he had something to do with real estate or was a close friend who came along because she didn't trust her prospective client. Sometimes it was too easy to get in a no-win situation.

Regardless of who thought what, she now had the listing. Ted seemed okay with that, not angry about Tyler, just smug that a problem arose concerning him. She suspected Ted's pride was hurt because she'd refused his invitations but accepted Tyler's and made it obvious at the picnic that she preferred Tyler over him.

She knew her tendency was to trust no one since George was unfaithful to her while they were engaged and even hit on one of her friends. She knew how easily a person could be drawn into activities that were wrong and unhealthy. She'd partied and done things in her teen years she wasn't proud of, so she could understand and forgive. But George had not been a teen when he proved not to love her the way she wanted to be loved. Now, when she thought she'd met an ideal man, questions kept cropping up.

Maybe she just needed to ask Tyler about his two years away. That could easily have been for higher education, teaching at another school, a trip around the world, or even a sabbatical. Leaving his sister with the Templetons could have been a decision he made according to what he thought was best for Penny.

Speculation!

That could lead to all kinds of problems. She didn't want to ask Ted to check out the rumors or converse about it with Ed Heffron. Bill was a policeman and didn't seem to be a strong Christian, but a growing one. He sat with Tyler during worship on Sunday. She didn't want to put negative thoughts in Bill's mind. And asking someone to check up on his friend wouldn't be right. Going to an attorney would be a terrible thing.

She'd already asked her aunt Eva about the Corbins. She'd known of their being in church but hadn't mingled with them personally. She had nothing negative to say, but everyone had been sorry about the accident that killed the parents. She'd heard Tyler was granted custody of Penny.

Why had he given that up to the Templetons? She could even understand he might have thought it best. She knew from having been a teenager that raising one wasn't the easiest thing in the world.

The morning dragged slowly. When the phone rang and Kay invited her to lunch, she readily accepted. Kay usually ate at the college cafeteria or in her office. This must be important. Fifteen minutes later she stood. "I'm going to lunch with Kay," she said.

Ted straightened and stared for a moment. "With Kay?"

Megan bristled. "Don't tell me you've heard rumors about Kay."

"Look, Megan." He stood and shoved his hands into his pockets. "Contrary to what you might think, I don't go around gossiping like a woman."

"Whoa!" Megan held out her hand.

He shook his head. "Sorry. I shouldn't have said that either.

What I'm trying to say is, I'm sorry I said anything about Tyler. Just forget it. Okay?"

"Sure," she said, knowing she couldn't although Ted did look contrite.

Walking over to the Veranda, she felt the warm summer sunshine on her face and breathed in the light breeze with fragrant smells. Jasmine grew alongside a brick building next to the parking lot. Pine gave off a fresh scent. Flowers were blooming in pots outside shops, and bushes along the sidewalks were sprouting new green leaves. She needed this respite from having negative thoughts about Tyler. Before now, everything about her relationship with Tyler had seemed positive.

Kay was waiting when Megan arrived. She sat at a table in the small alcove near the windows facing Cherry Street, away from the main eating area.

Walking to the table, Megan smiled. "You must have left the college right after you called."

"I was ready to go." Her smile was friendly as always.

Carrie, the waitress, came right over. After speaking with her for a moment, Megan ordered the flavored tea. Kay asked for sweet tea. They both ordered salad and a cup of soup.

As soon as Carrie left with their order, Megan was about to tell Kay about the Heffron contract, but Kay was fingering the napkin that covered the silverware. When she looked across at Megan, something serious lay in her eyes.

"I'm not sure how to do this," Kay said.

Kay wasn't one to talk personally. Megan waited, sending up a silent prayer she might say and do the right things, if only to listen.

"About the picnic," Kay began.

Megan nodded. She knew of only one picnic.

"Ted and I were talking. . . ."

Oh, no. Had Ted said something about Tyler that Kay thought she should warn her about? Instead of asking, she merely nodded for Kay to continue. "Are you, I mean, is there something special between you and Tyler?"

Apparently there shouldn't be. "I had thought that might happen," Megan admitted.

Kay glanced around, then finally met her eyes. "Megan, I know you've talked about Ted asking you out and making insinuations."

Megan didn't think she could stand any more. "Kay, just come out and say it. What did Ted say? I can take it."

Kay closed her eyes and spoke through a grimace. "He asked me out."

He asked her out? That was it?

"Kay." The relief Megan felt bubbled up, and she feared she'd laugh out loud. She picked up her napkin and covered her mouth. She cleared her throat and tried not to laugh. "What did you tell him?"

"I said I'd think about it."

Megan took a deep breath. "So you want my opinion of him?"

Kay looked across at her with soulful eyes. "I think I know your opinion of him. You've always said he's a nice guy but not your type. I just. . .need to be sure."

Kay and Ted?

That laughter started to bubble again. "You want my approval?"

"Well, I wouldn't if there's a chance for you and him. That's why I asked about Tyler."

Megan could honestly report on that. "I don't know yet

about Tyler. But I do know about Ted and me. There's nothing between us and can never be. I'd never thought about the possibility of you and him."

"I wouldn't have either. But at the picnic we got to talking personally. He said he'd accepted Jesus into his heart when he was a child, but he'd let life and a broken marriage bring bitterness into his heart. He even said you have made a difference in his life."

"Me?" Megan had thought he just wanted to run around and have a good time.

Kay nodded. "Your involvement in church and your faithfulness to the Lord have had an impact on him, and he was trying to ignore that. But"—Kay spoke softly—"I believe he's being convicted about committing his life to the Lord."

Megan could understand that was a real possibility. "Kay, I think that's great."

Kay breathed a sigh of relief. They both relaxed and welcomed Carrie when she brought their lunch. Megan took a sip of her ginger-peach tea, then began eating the salad that seemed to be even tastier than usual.

After lunch when she returned to the office, Megan pretended not to notice Ted's curious glances. "How was lunch?" he asked.

"We went to the Veranda. It's always good."

"Hmm."

She went to her desk, answered a phone call, and checked her e-mail.

"How's Kay?"

"Good."

"Hmm."

She didn't have a napkin to cover her mouth this time, and

it was almost more than she could do not to laugh. Finally she looked at him and said, "Ted, just ask it."

His face colored. "Okay, okay. Did Kay mention me?"

"Yep."

He leaned his head back and gazed at the ceiling. "You're torturing me."

"Well," Megan quipped, "I think what Kay had to say is your own personal business."

He faced her then. When she smiled, the question in his eyes turned to hope, then acceptance. Instead of his finger touching his nose, it touched his chest. "My. . .business?"

Megan shrugged. "That's what I said."

"Oh. Hmm. Well, touché." He suddenly looked contrite. "And, Megan. I'm sorry I'm sometimes a lout. Just forget anything I've said about Tyler."

Nodding, she told herself that's exactly what she'd planned to do all along. But as the day dragged so did her inability to forget.

ten

Tyler looked up from his real estate book when Penny came in from work. Before he could even ask how her day went, she plopped down in a chair opposite him in the family room. She had an expectant look on her face. "I'm off tomorrow," she said. "What about my asking Megan to come over for grilled steaks or something?"

His eyebrows lifted. "You're courting Megan now?"

"Tyler, don't be obtuse." Her voice held feigned exasperation. "I just want to thank her for the gift card she gave me."

"Oh," he said. "You received several gifts and a few cards with money in them. So does that mean we'll have a dozen or so people here for dinner?"

"No–o–o—just Megan. After all, I haven't known her a long time, and it was sweet of her to give me such a nice gift. I thought dinner would be a good way to thank her."

"Fine." He lowered his eyes to his book. "I'll make myself scarce." He pretended to read, waiting for her outburst.

Finally he heard her sigh. "Okay, smarty-pants. So you know what I'm up to." She stood. "You've been home every night for over a week except when you go to A-B Tech for your real estate class. Then you have your nose poked in a book. I'm afraid if you don't show more interest in Megan she'll find somebody else."

Tyler closed the book and looked at it for a long moment, thinking how to respond. At the last real estate class, the instructor had told them to take the offense instead of defense. When a client finds something wrong with a property, that's his cue to point out something positive or change the subject. Get the person's mind on something else. He'd try to divert Penny with her questions and observations.

He leaned forward, his elbows on his book. "What about you, little sister? All I see you doing is working seven to three, going to the supermarket, cooking, cleaning. I haven't noticed your having any kind of social life."

"Well, it seems to me my big brother said I should finish college before getting serious about a guy." She wore a triumphant expression. Yes, he'd said that years ago when she wasn't listening to him about anything. It figured that now she'd remember it. "But you." She wagged a finger at him. "You have a beautiful woman who likes you, and you ignore her. No woman can take that for long."

Tyler knew she was right. Trying to keep a woman interested and at a distance at the same time presented a dilemma. And, too, he'd begun to want to see her. He'd hoped the memory of her in his arms and the touch of his lips on hers would fade, but it persisted. "Call her," he said.

"Um, would you?" Penny feigned an innocent look. "Since you know her better?"

28

"Tyler?" Hearing his voice on the phone lifted Megan's spirits. She'd begun to think he'd never call. Every time the phone rang it was like a spark of electricity, igniting something inside her. Would it be Tyler? When it wasn't, she reminded herself she'd decided to take things slowly with any man, if she ever got interested in one. She hadn't counted on that chance meeting with someone like Tyler.

Nor had she counted on the feeling of excitement when she saw him or thought of him. She was going to take things slowly, but when Tyler went so long without contacting her she felt abandoned again. That wasn't the feeling she'd expected to have. She'd resolved that being alone was what she wanted, needed, for a long time. Then along came Tyler, and her resolution was dissolving, against her will.

Her spirits plummeted, however, when he said Penny wanted her to come to dinner as a thank-you for the gift card. A part of her wanted to jump at the chance to be with Tyler. Another part wondered if he wanted her there. Why didn't he say so? She decided to hedge. "Tomorrow night? Let me check my calendar."

She checked her mental calendar which told her she had no evening appointments. "My calendar is clear tomorrow night. I'd love to have dinner with Penny."

She smiled at the phone when he said, "I'll be there, too. You like your steak medium well, right?" So he remembered how she'd ordered her steak cooked at the Bistro. She felt her smile fade when he added, "I have a few real estate questions I'd like to discuss with you."

⁂

All the way to Tyler and Penny's home, Megan kept telling herself this was a friendly visit. Just as she'd decided long ago that a relationship with any man would have to be on a friends-only basis, she had to keep reminding herself this relationship with Tyler was friends-only, too. She certainly wasn't ready for serious thoughts, and why she had them was beyond her. She hardly knew the man. And the fact that she didn't go around kissing men she didn't care for a lot didn't mean Tyler held that same view about kissing women.

Megan stepped up onto the porch, past the rocking chairs where she and Tyler had sat briefly the day they met, when she brought him and Penny a fruit basket. She rang the bell. When Penny opened the door, Megan couldn't help but feel relaxed and welcomed by Penny's bright smile.

"Tyler's almost finished with the steaks. Everything else is done, so would you like a tour of the house while we're waiting? Who knows? You might be called upon to list it someday."

Was he planning to sell the house? Her heart skipped a beat, thinking he had said he wanted to talk to her about real estate. Maybe he was planning to sell his house. Was he planning to move away? He'd been gone two years. Was he planning to return to wherever he'd come from? Her curiosity was stirred.

"Since Tyler is studying real estate, he would probably list it himself, don't you think?"

"Oh, I guess you're right."

"All the same I'd love a tour," Megan said.

Penny gestured toward the staircase. "Well, there's really no need to look upstairs. Those are just bedrooms. I still have the same one I always had. When I was young and foolish, I complained about his being up there when I had friends over. I wanted the upstairs all to myself and my friends. Now that I don't have friends spend the night, I have the entire upstairs. Go figure."

Megan laughed at Penny's assessment. "I know what you mean. When I was a teen, I thought having a car like the one I have, a good job, and independence was the ultimate goal. Now that I have them I have to work to make those car payments, and I still have to answer to someone. And I found out independence isn't all it's cracked up to be."

Penny's ponytail swung around as she turned her head. "Yeah. But I've learned those are not the important things in life. Without a relationship with the Lord, nothing in life has meaning."

"So true," Megan said. But shouldn't she, being older, be the one to say that? Penny appeared to be quite mature for her age. Maybe losing her parents had caused her to mature spiritually.

The living room was formal, as she would expect of a house in this area, as was the dining room with its large picture window and the chandelier hanging above a table that would seat eight or ten comfortably.

The family room was less formal. Penny spoke in a wistful tone. "Tyler and my dad both liked to use the family room for just about everything, from grading papers to reading. We used to play a lot of games, too."

Megan could imagine winters in particular when the family would curl up on the big, well-cushioned couch that faced the fireplace.

They walked down the hallway, and Penny pointed out the location of the master bedroom which Tyler occupied. They didn't go in there but continued to the kitchen.

"I like the way Mom had this room renovated," Penny said. "She tried to teach me to cook, but I didn't care much back then. Beth Templeton taught me when I lived with them, and I was much more interested."

Megan could see this would be a great kitchen to cook in. It boasted granite countertops and the latest in cabinet design, conveniently placed appliances, and an island ideal for informal eating. But what she liked most was the view of the patio from beyond the windows.

Tyler stood in front of a grill, testing the steaks with a long fork. The patio was surrounded by a brick wall about three feet high. Above the wall were shrubs and trees almost obscuring glimpses of other nearby houses. Her attention gravitated, though, to Tyler, who forked steaks onto a dish, covered them with a lid, and headed for the sliding glass doors.

He was all smiles when he came inside and saw her. His look made her feel special. "Megan, welcome. I see you wore your favorite color." She'd worn casual dress slacks and a red silk blouse simply because he'd commented on her liking red.

"It wasn't when I was a child. My hair was lighter then. I was really a carrottop and was teased unmercifully about my red hair. Particularly by Bobby, a classmate whose goal in life seemed to be to embarrass me. He'd tease me, then say my cheeks turned as red as my hair when I got angry."

"But haven't you heard a person only teases someone they like?" He grinned and glanced at the table. "In case you were not wearing red this evening, I have a red rose for you. That color suits you." He deliberately cleared his throat. "Whether it's on your head or in your cheeks."

His playfulness put her at ease, although she did feel the warmth, likely accompanied by color, in her face. She lifted her chin. "I'll bet you say that to all the girls." Gesturing toward the vase she said, "I see three roses in that vase. Apparently you have two other redheads in your life."

She really colored then. How could she be so silly to imply she was "in his life"?

He obviously didn't think anything of what she said. He smiled. "The other two are for important people in my life.

But not redheads. One is for Penny in case I ruined the steaks and therefore her dinner. The other is for me." He poked his chest. "Because no one ever gives me roses."

"Oh, sad," wailed Penny.

All three laughed, but at the sound of Penny's voice, Megan realized she'd forgotten the younger girl was in the room. It had seemed to be only she and Tyler. Now she noticed Penny had set a salad bowl at each place and a baked potato on the plates with an orange slice for color. "Time for the steaks, Ty."

"By the way," Megan said, "your hat is most becoming."

"Oh." His hand went to his chef's hat. "I did that to convince you I can cook. Forgot I was wearing it." He laid it on the island.

He forgot? The same reason she had forgotten Penny?

Penny lit the candles while Tyler forked the steaks onto plates and deposited the platter on the island. He then pulled out a chair. "Sit here and you'll have a good view of the patio."

"She'll have a view of the grill," Penny said, smiling.

"I could move it," he said, after Megan was seated and he had pulled out the chair for his sister.

"Don't do that," Megan protested. "I've seen it. Grills are among my favorite cooking appliances. Are they appliances?"

They laughed. No one knew.

"Maybe contraptions," Tyler said.

After they laughed again, he lowered his head. Megan and Penny closed their eyes, and he thanked God that Megan could join them and asked His blessings upon the food.

The conversation was light—about books they'd read and music they liked, plus interesting things that happened with Tyler at the juvenile center, Megan in real estate, and Penny at the conference center.

After dinner Megan offered to help with the dishes, but Penny wouldn't let her. "Tyler can clean the grill later. I'll take care of things in here." She rose from her chair. "Ty, I gave Megan a tour of the house. Why don't you give her a tour of the outside?"

Megan would prefer that Tyler suggest it, but she reminded herself this was Penny's thank-you dinner, not his. Regardless, she liked the feeling of being alone with him on the patio, particularly when he said, "I'm glad you came tonight, Megan. She is a thoughtful, generous girl, but she has the heart of a matchmaker when it comes to me."

"Really?" Megan said. "Well, I'm flattered. But—doesn't she think you can find your own women?"

"That's not it." He glanced around, then back. "She's afraid I'll lose you by going too slow."

"What do you think?"

He took a deep breath; then his beautiful eyes gazed into hers, and her heart had no idea what *slow* meant.

"I don't want to lose you, Megan. But I do need to take things slowly right now. Because of things in the past, I can't jump into something."

A light laugh escaped Megan. "I've told myself the same thing. But I haven't been sure you were interested—"

"Interested?" he interrupted. "In you?"

She nodded, knowing her smile was weak.

"Megan, I've been interested from the time I saw that beautiful woman on the side of the road, kicking the tire of a red sports car with the toe of a high-heeled shoe. That was a rare sight, like seeing a bright red cardinal. I hoped you wouldn't flit away as a bird startled by someone's presence."

"I'm not startled, Tyler." She laughed.

He spread his hands, looking like a reprimanded kid. "I was trying to make a creative analogy."

"It was a beautiful one and"—she tilted her head to the side—"creative. . .original." She thought it might be wise to flit away or at least change the subject and try to look away from his mesmerizing gaze. She glanced away for a moment, then back. "Seriously though, Tyler, I still have healing to do from my past. I should take things slowly."

"Slow it is," he said. "Now, if it pleases you, how about our taking a brisk walk around Lake Tomahawk?"

eleven

Joggers and walkers frequented the half-mile path around Lake Tomahawk. No swimming was allowed, but a couple of small boys sat on the bank, casting their fishing lines for the rainbow trout and bass that made the lake their home.

Tyler and Megan didn't jog or walk briskly, though; they took it slow. Their glances met and their smiles matched as they passed the sand-filled play area where children screamed joyfully while sliding down the chute, hanging on monkey bars, making sandcastles, and swinging.

Off to the right, children were taking grain from a bin to feed the ducks. Tyler stopped to look at the little ones who were tentatively watching as ducks swam close.

"You must like children," Megan said, "since you teach them."

"Very much. I always thought it would be great to have a brother or at least a sibling close to my age when growing up. I fell in love with Penny from the moment she was born, but I was always the big brother. We couldn't communicate on the same level."

"You seem to communicate well now," Megan said as they walked along the hard-packed dirt path. "Of course, you know more than she does."

He nodded. "I have more education and more life experience in a way. But she's had a hard time since Mom and Dad were killed. She's growing into a remarkable young woman, intent upon serving the Lord and using her life productively."

"She does seem to be remarkable," Megan agreed.

Tyler smiled. "Only thing is, our roles seem to have reversed. She now thinks she needs to mother me. Speaking of mothering, how about you? What do you think of children?"

"I love them. I had a sister and cousins growing up. Now my sister is married with three children of her own, so there's not a lot of time for getting together except on holidays. Our family sort of fell apart after Dad left us. That did a lot of damage. And when I was dating George, we talked about children but both wanted to wait until we could give them everything." They stepped off to the side when a woman neared them, pushing a buggy with two small children in it. He saw the tender look in Megan's eyes as she watched them.

"Now," she said, "I think that was based on selfishness. It wasn't what we wanted for children, but what we wanted for ourselves. Children need love most, not things."

As they walked beneath the overhanging limbs of lofty pines, Tyler reminisced. "You're so right. Penny and I never lacked for the things you speak of. But after our parents died three years ago, we would have traded all that to have them back. I tried, but I couldn't replace them in Penny's life."

"Is that why you sent her to the Templetons?"

Fortunately they came to a grade where their steps became slower as they ascended it. That gave him a moment to think how to answer, while still being truthful. They smiled at each other after looking to the right where two young boys sat with tackle boxes, casting their fishing lines into the water.

"Catch anything?" Tyler asked, walking over.

"Got a rainbow trout here," one of them said.

Tyler stepped over and looked.

"I caught a big bass," the other said, spreading his hands to show how big, "but it got away."

"Keep trying." Tyler returned to Megan on the path. He still had to answer her question. "I wanted Penny to have the best. I couldn't give her parents, but the Templetons were good for her. Ah, hear the music."

Megan looked ahead, but he saw the reserved look on her face, as if she were thinking about his answer, not the music.

He stepped behind her to let a jogger pass. After they had continued in silence for a while, she finally spoke. "Did you leave town to take another teaching job?"

He took a deep breath, then exhaled. They neared the bridge over the creek that ran into the lake. Off to the left was a group of people in lawn chairs and on blankets, some sitting on the grass, listening to four guys picking guitars and singing country songs. Seemingly without prying, she kept asking questions pointing to those two years.

They stopped on the wide bridge that had a four-foot-high stone wall on each side. Tyler rested his forearms on the top, and for a moment he watched the cold creek water flow from under the bridge into the lake. "Water under the bridge" was an adage that crossed his mind. He thought the saying applied to something being over and forgotten. Now it took on a new meaning. Like that creek water, the past didn't stay hidden away. In life sometimes the past could stay there. Other times it simply flowed out to become part of a larger picture.

He needed to be as honest as he could. "Megan, there is something I can't tell you." Tyler kept watching the water flow into the lake. "I can only ask you to trust that I'm not some kind of villain." He suspected she had heard things about him, or maybe she just wanted to know why he didn't speak of some things.

After a couple passed by, he turned to face her. "People get to know each other by finding out about their past, their likes, dislikes. But there are things I can't talk about yet. More important than where I've been or what I've done is the present. I'm asking you to take me at face value."

She seemed to study him with questions in her eyes. Finally she nodded but turned to look at the lake with a serious expression on her face.

He wondered how that would go over with her. He wanted to know everything about her—her past, her thoughts, her feelings, her dreams. But he could settle for what he knew.

Suddenly she interrupted his thoughts. "I'd better get back for that red rose and then go home. Have to work tomorrow."

"I've enjoyed this, Megan," he said as they walked back to his car.

"So have I," she said.

They were relatively quiet on the return to the house. He hadn't asked an easy thing of her. When they reached the house, Megan went inside to thank Penny again for the dinner.

By the time Tyler wrapped the rose stem in a wet tissue and handed it to Megan, Penny had made herself scarce.

After walking Megan to her car, Tyler handed her the rose. He wanted to bend closer and touch his lips to hers. He thought she wouldn't have minded. But they both needed to know if she could take him at face value. "I enjoyed being with you this evening, Megan."

"Me, too," she said softly.

Take it slow, he reminded himself and stepped back as

Megan said good night.

Much later he tried to think of the evening, what they'd said and done and his growing feelings for her. He prayed for God's will in his choice of a life's mate. His own will was Megan. He had to pray that if this wasn't God's choice for him, then the relationship wouldn't go forward. But tonight had been good. They'd learned how each felt about children. They both liked being together and agreed to go slow.

He thought of his last view of her tonight. She had smelled the red rose and laid it on the seat beside her. Then he watched her in her red silk blouse, driving away in her bright red car.

The pleasant thoughts ended with a more serious one. He'd asked her to take him at face value.

What was his face value from her viewpoint? He was a man who admitted he had given his sister over to another couple while she was still a teenager. He had secrets about which he wouldn't talk.

Face value? If she thought about it, she'd probably never see him again.

❧

Now that Ted was interested in Kay, Megan had thought his ability to ruin her day had ended. Was his relationship with Kay going sour and he was back to needling her? All she'd said was, "Tyler's coming along quite well with his real estate studies. He has a knack for it and knows the area. He's well aware of the importance of location." She added, "You might even want him working for you."

Ted's head moved from side to side, and he glared at her. "I'm sorry, but I can't even consider that, Megan."

She should never have said anything. "He might not even

want to work for you, Ted. I was merely speaking a thought out loud."

"Well, it's out of the question."

She stared at him. "Why?"

He looked concerned. "I know everybody in town, Megan. You know that. I hear things."

"What things?"

"It's not for me to say." His fingers lifted to the tip of his nose.

Anger rose in her. "But it's for you to insinuate and make comments to make me think I need to beware of Tyler. Look, Ted. I've seen him several times. We've met a few times to discuss real estate. He's a perfect gentleman."

He shook his head. "This has nothing to do with being a gentleman. He seems like a great guy. That's why I was jealous because you wouldn't go out with me but you would with him." He lifted his hand. "But that's over. I know you're not interested in me that way."

Megan walked over to his desk. "Why don't you just tell me what you've heard?"

He looked up at her, his gaze serious. "Because I've heard several things. And some speculation. Some just ask questions about his having been away. If you want to know, ask him." He shrugged. "Or check him out."

Megan turned and walked to her desk, looked at the computer, and brought up real estate Web sites. She didn't really see what appeared on the screen.

Ask him.

She'd tried, but Tyler wanted her to take him at face value.

What did she know of him? He attended church. He taught young boys at the juvenile center. He loved his sister.

He had made repairs for the Templetons. He'd taken a group out to celebrate Penny's first year of college. He was friendly, confident, handsome, intelligent, educated. And he wanted to take the relationship slowly. Those were admirable traits.

She thought of the rose. He liked flowers—liked to plant them and give them. His sister thought enough of him to live in the house with him, and Penny obviously loved and respected him.

She didn't want the doubts Ted's words embedded in her mind. But she couldn't help but wonder why Tyler wouldn't speak of the two years he was away. Maybe he was ashamed of things he'd done in the past. But so was she, for that matter.

Was he divorced and didn't want to talk about it?

The thought occurred to her that he might not want to consider a serious relationship while Penny was still young and single. She'd had a hard time after losing her parents. He was being a parent to her. Maybe he thought Penny would feel like an outsider if he began seeing someone seriously. But that didn't make sense, because he said Penny was trying to be a matchmaker for them.

"Check him out," Ted had said.

How? Hire a private detective? She laughed aloud at that.

"Something funny?" Ted asked.

She shrugged. "Not funny enough to repeat." She again tried to concentrate on the screen. She didn't need a detective to know how Tyler spent his time. He taught five mornings a week at the center and attended a real estate class three nights a week at A-B Tech.

She said a silent prayer for God to intervene if there was some reason for her to be concerned about Tyler—if he was not right for her, for her to know that. She truly wanted

God's will in His choice for a life's mate. She had not asked that when going with George. But she knew living in God's will was the only way to make a marriage work.

Marriage? Oh, my. She shouldn't be thinking of marriage to a man who made it clear he wanted to go slow. Or maybe he was simply stating his moral standard? When he said "take it slow," was he referring to a physical relationship? Letting her know he lived up to his Christian commitment?

Well, if so, that was certainly commendable.

No, she would do as Tyler asked and take him at face value. She would not check him out. But it suddenly came to her what to do about those unfounded insinuations of Ted's.

When he left the office to show a property, Megan took her cell phone from her purse. She knew the person who would erase any doubts Ted had implanted in her mind.

She punched in the numbers.

twelve

Megan couldn't go to the Templetons, because they might tell Tyler she had asked questions about him. But she admired and respected Pastor Wrend and felt he would never divulge that she sought counseling concerning Tyler. A pastor, like a psychiatrist or psychologist, was bound by confidentiality.

That's what he said after they dispensed with courtesy talk of asking about each other's families and health, the weather, and a general state of being. Finally he smiled kindly. "Now, Megan, what can I do for you?"

"Well, first, maybe I should say a little about my background. My former fiancé proved to be untrustworthy, so I'm trying to be cautious before allowing myself to get serious with any man."

He nodded, smiling.

How could she ever ease into this? "And I know scripture says not to be 'yoked together with unbelievers.'"

Another brief nod indicated she was doing fine so far. "I'm seeing someone now. He seems to be a wonderful person, but. . .I've. . .heard rumors."

Only for an instant did his gaze lock with hers; then his eyelids lowered. If she hadn't been watching for a reaction, she could have missed it. She felt he knew who she was talking about. He looked at her again, though, almost expressionless. "Go on."

Watching him closely, she continued. "This person has

asked me to take him at face value. People keep insinuating things about him, but when I try to ask him about his past, he skirts the issue. I'm afraid I should be concerned about something in his past."

Pastor Wrend turned his head to gaze out the window. Finally he looked at her again. "I think I know who you're referring to. But you'll have to tell me."

"Tyler Corbin."

His nod indicated he was not surprised. "This is not the first time I've been questioned about him since his return." His gaze penetrated her. "Others have heard rumors also, and most of them are far from the truth."

Megan felt a stirring in her stomach. "So there is something."

He leaned forward slightly. "Megan, as a pastor, I'm sworn to confidentiality. I can't tell anyone what I know about another person. Just as I can't tell anyone what you and I talk about today. Would you want to tell me what you heard?"

Megan hesitated. "It's all vague. I don't know anyone who knew him personally. But one person said she heard he was in some kind of trouble. Another said he lost custody of his sister and the Templetons became her foster parents. Another just keeps telling me I should check him out."

"So that's what you're doing."

Now was her time to nod. She felt ready to cry. There was something, but the pastor wasn't going to tell her. She felt worse than if she hadn't made this appointment. She stared at her hands in her lap.

"Megan," he said kindly.

She looked up, hardly meeting his gaze.

"I can tell you this, which is what I have to say to most—we are all sinners. We all sin and make mistakes. If most of us were judged by something we did, usually in our teen years when we're beginning to learn about life, then none of us could be respected. That's what change and forgiveness are all about. As we mature, we should be striving to live a life pleasing to the Lord."

She made a feeble attempt to smile.

"I will say this also, Megan. You can take Tyler Corbin at face value. Knowing him has taught me firsthand that we need to be careful about judging. Things are not always what they seem. Sometimes they are what they seem, and we need to forgive and move on."

He waited until she looked directly at him. He spoke confidently. "Tyler Corbin is one of the finest men I've ever known. He's a trustworthy person. I hope you can take my word for that. I'm sworn to confidentiality, so I can't say what I'd like to. But I'd bet my life on Tyler Corbin. Incidentally," he said, his smile reaching his eyes, "I think you and Tyler would make a great pair."

She felt her cheeks grow warm. "Thank you." She stood, and so did he. They shook hands.

Megan sat in her car for quite a while in the church parking lot. She felt good about Pastor Wrend's high appraisal of Tyler. And yet the conversation did the opposite of what she'd hoped. She'd wanted to be assured nothing terrible was in Tyler's past.

Now she was convinced something was there.

Where could she go from here?

But should she allow herself to become serious with Tyler if he wouldn't confide in her? Was she setting herself up for heartbreak again?

What tugged at her the most was the phrase "Tyler was

away for two years." What did that mean? When she spoke of her sister, she said, "Janet married and moved to the suburbs." When Tyler spoke of his parents, he said, "They died. They were killed." When her family explained her, they said, "She lives with her aunt Eva in Black Mountain." Who ever spoke of someone being "away"?

Dread engulfed her.

Let it go, kept running through her mind.

But her little red car turned toward the interstate and west to Asheville.

She hated to do it, but she drove to the courthouse and asked for Tyler Corbin's record. She could hardly believe the information she was given. As if in a daze, she went to the newspaper office and asked to see back copies of newspapers with the dates of the incident reported in the courthouse records. She found the articles about his being arrested for stealing a car, having an open container of alcohol, crashing, and worst of all, being in possession of drugs. He refused a breathalyzer test, was taken to jail, pled guilty, and was eventually sentenced to Craggy Correctional Center and community service upon his release.

He pled guilty.

That meant he was guilty, didn't it?

And—he wasn't teaching at the juvenile center because he cared about those boys. He was teaching because the court required it.

After finding out about Tyler's past, Megan had no idea what to do or how to think. Maybe Tyler was right in saying she needed to take him at face value as far as what he was doing presently. She tried to evaluate that in light of what she knew now. He attended church and was taking a summer course in real estate. She had believed he liked teaching at the juvenile center when he told her about it, but that wasn't his decision. Would he teach there if the court hadn't demanded it? A person's past shouldn't be held against him if he changes. But a person is made up of his—or her—past, too.

Maybe he could explain it. Had he gotten in with the wrong crowd? Become involved before he realized it? Why was he in possession of drugs? Did he buy them? Did someone else put them in the car? The record said the car was stolen. Maybe he didn't know the drugs were there?

Stole a car?

Why would he steal a car? It's not as if he were a teenager without a car. This was two years ago. He was a mature man, out of college, teaching school, so he would have been twenty-seven or twenty-eight. An intelligent, educated man couldn't just get caught up in something like that. It had to be deliberate.

But there had to be an explanation.

She could understand he wouldn't want to talk about such a thing. Maybe that's why he said he wanted to take their relationship slow. He wouldn't want to confide in everyone about a shameful past. But if the two of them were going to get serious, she would have to know about something like this.

She'd known of people who never seemed to get over a drug addiction. Had Tyler been addicted? Could she chance such a thing?

Many people likely knew about his past. The pastor did. Everyone seemed to think highly of him. But Ted had tried to warn her.

Had Tyler taken a job as teacher so he could be near unsuspecting young children and sell drugs? Oh, the thought was horrendous.

When she went to the office the following day, she told Ted, "I took your advice and checked up on Tyler." She faced her computer, trying to appear emotionless.

Finally he said, "So did I."

Megan closed her eyes until the sinking feeling subsided. What could she say? Ted could gloat now.

He didn't gloat but simply said, "It's hard to believe."

Megan nodded. "There has to be an explanation."

Ted walked to the middle of the floor. He looked concerned, not triumphant. "Megan, I admit I was irritated when you wouldn't go out with me but would with him. That's a male ego thing."

He grinned, so she did, too, although she was far from feeling anything akin to humor. He grew serious then. "But you know, Megan, anytime someone does something that seems to be out of character, people always say they never suspected, never would have thought it, are shocked. I know that's how you must feel." He shook his head. "I'm honestly not trying to condemn him. I've not exactly been an angel myself."

Megan nodded. She knew people could do things that even surprised them. "But this seems so out of character for him."

Ted was being okay about this. "Maybe it is now. Maybe that incident straightened him out. I don't want to get into my own sordid private life that led to divorce, but losing my wife and having the children part-time brought me to my senses in a hurry, though too late."

"Oh, Ted. We shouldn't go around talking about it."

He was already shaking his head. "I won't. I wouldn't want you or anybody doing that to me, especially now that I'm seeing Kay. But"—he had that concerned look again—"I suspect people know about Tyler. But maybe not. I don't recall seeing anything in the newspaper or on TV."

"I saw the newspaper article," she said. "But it wasn't in a prominent place in the paper."

Megan thought about Ted's saying he wouldn't want rumors going around about him so he'd show the same consideration for Tyler. Ted would reserve his personal disclosures for the person he would be serious with. That's how she felt. She would like for her relationship with Tyler to continue. But how could she, knowing what she knew—unless he explained it satisfactorily.

What if there were no valid explanations? He couldn't claim being young and foolish as an excuse.

But all the speculation in the world wasn't giving her the answers.

When Tyler called and asked if she'd like to go out to dinner on Friday night at the Cellar Door, she accepted. "That's the ritzy place, right?"

"It's upscale, but I doubt they'd throw us out for being casual."

"I wouldn't want to chance it, Tyler. So I'll dress for the occasion."

She felt like this was a special occasion, perhaps a turning point in her feeling torn between taking him at face value as he had asked and getting to the truth. If they were not meant to have a future together, she at least wanted closure, not some haunting question of what might have been.

thirteen

Tyler wondered if he was making too much of a trite thing, but the color red had become a game she played with him. Or that's what he had thought. Once he joked that he was disappointed she wasn't wearing that color. She'd grinned, held out her arm, and showed him her bracelet where a couple of red charms dangled. Another time she gave him a coy glance, accompanied by a grin, and smoothed her hair back from her face, revealing rubies in her earrings. He liked that little playful game.

When he went to the door on Friday evening, she said her aunt Eva had gone out with friends, so she didn't invite him in. He studied her as they walked to the car, and he held the car door while she settled into the passenger seat.

His perusal was not only to discover the absence of the color red but also to notice how nice she looked in the silky ivory-colored dress that flowed with her movements, instead of her tailored look as a Realtor. Her jewelry was gold, including her watchband, bracelet, and rings. He saw no red. Her heels were higher than the ones she wore to work. He couldn't imagine how a woman walked in such high heels and with only thin straps across her feet. That thought was offset by the elegant turn of her ankles and bare legs. Her toenails were painted a peachy color, like her fingernails.

He warned himself not to stare too long. "You look lovely," he said.

"Thank you." Her glossy peach-colored lips were, at the moment, more intriguing than the rest of her. "You cleaned up pretty well yourself."

"You mean the tie matches?"

"Perfectly."

Nodding, he closed the car door. He tried to complement such a beautiful woman with his clothing, but a man could do only so much with a suit and different colored shirts. With the help of store clerks, and sometimes Penny, he managed to match, complete with a silk handkerchief in the breast pocket upon occasion, such as tonight.

Taking his place at the wheel, Tyler's glance swept over her again. He grinned. "You're not wearing red."

She didn't laugh or joke about it but simply said, "No, I'm not wearing red."

Well, of course that was fine. He turned the key in the ignition and backed out of the driveway onto Montreat Road. Was she tired of the game, or did he detect a modicum of tension when his glance revealed her looking at the scenery?

"Nice evening," he said.

"Mmm-hmm," she agreed.

On the three-minute drive to the restaurant, he saw that the scenery was nice but no different from other pleasant summer evenings. They were making only casual conversation, though. Something inside him quickened with the thought that the evening might not remain casual. When people dressed formally the mood often accompanied it. Maybe his imagination was working overtime simply because she wasn't wearing red.

But he knew, no matter how hard he tried to convince himself otherwise, if all were okay, she would have joked about the color. Some couples had favorite songs, special movies, meaningful places to go. They'd had the color red.

Until now.

He shouldn't be so sensitive as to think something so insignificant as red or a three-minute contemplative mood had anything to do with him. This was part of getting to know each other, wasn't it? Learning what bothered a person, talking it over, understanding.

The maître d' seated them at a corner table, as he'd requested when making the reservation, so they could be fairly private. The waitress came immediately to take their beverage order.

He watched Megan look around at the paneled walls, pendant lights, dark cherry tables. "I like this setting," she said. "I've only been here once for lunch." Her smile held approval.

Tyler had already checked it out. "I brought Penny here one night. She said it was elegant and romantic."

Why couldn't Megan have given him one of those long, lingering looks that conveyed warmth as she had done a few times in the past? Perhaps this was not the occasion for that. Maybe their agreement to take things slowly meant to her they were not to speak of romance. If so, then she shouldn't look so attractive.

After the waitress brought their drinks and took their order, they engaged in small talk of how each had been, how the week had gone, how Aunt Eva and Penny were doing.

When their salads were set in front of them Tyler reached across to hold her hand and say the blessing. When he finished, Megan didn't meet his gaze but gently pulled her hand away and picked up her silverware.

Silence could be comfortable. This was not the case. They

agreed the salad and house dressing were quite good. After taking a few bites she laid her fork down and blotted her lips. "Tyler?" The way she said his name sounded like a question.

He was tasting the balsamic vinaigrette dressing but had the feeling something more sour than vinegar was about to occur.

"You know I care about you or I wouldn't be seeing you."

Instinct told him this wasn't light banter and didn't call for a response on his part. She hesitated, as if she might be reluctant to say whatever was on her mind. He'd said they should go slow. Was she about to say they should come to a screeching halt?

"I think," she said, "if we're going to keep seeing each other, we should learn to know each other better."

Having salad in his mouth, he simply nodded. But he feared what that might mean.

She chewed and swallowed a bite of salad, then took a sip of water. "What I mean is, I'd like you to know what kind of person I was as a child, a teen, an adult."

"I think I know what kind of adult you are," he said.

"Not really," she said. "My favorite color isn't red. It's. . .it's blue."

He knew that, too, from a conversation they'd had the first Sunday he'd gone into the welcome room after church. He jested. "No-o-o. You misled me. How am I supposed to deal with such deception?"

At least his overacting made her laugh. He laughed along with her but had a feeling their laughter was shallow.

He nodded. "We learn more about one another each time we're together. But I think you have something more specific in mind."

"Tyler, I've told you I have a hard time trusting men since my dad and my fiancé both disappointed me. I think for a relationship to thrive, two people need to be totally honest. Don't you?"

The waitress came then with their entrées—hers, the filet mignon; his, the ribeye steak. After each took a bite, they acknowledged the food was delicious. In this tense moment Tyler didn't feel it was the time to ask if they should exchange bites of food as they had at the Bistro. Apparently neither did Megan.

Tyler had assumed the tension was because of his not telling her about his past. Now it suddenly occurred to him her mood might have something to do with her past that she feared revealing.

"Megan," he said, "I don't think people have to go into detail about everything they've ever done wrong."

"I don't mean that," she said. "But I think we have to be honest about the important things. Don't you?"

"Sure. I believe honesty is important. If either of us has a troubled past that needs attention, then it should be addressed. But I don't think we need to tell every detail."

She was eating her food, but he had the impression she wasn't enjoying it. After a moment she said, "Some details are important, Tyler."

She began to tell some things she'd done that she wasn't proud of. He tried to stop her, but she insisted. "If I demand honesty from others, then I must be honest about myself."

He listened as she told about her teen years, too much partying at times, things that had gotten out of hand. Her confessions were mild compared to what they might have been. She knew that and said by the grace of God she'd been protected from some things that could have ruined her life. She spoke of her difficulties with her family, her harsh feelings about her former fiancé and his untrustworthiness.

Tyler could easily relate his own sins, things he'd done or wanted to do and hadn't. "All that is forgiven, Megan. I still sin whether it's by commission, omission, or an unguarded thought. But I try to live daily for the Lord. Living the Christian life is a daily effort."

"Oh, Tyler. I want to believe that. And I would love to take you at face value, because I believe you are a fine, Christian man. But I've been hurt. I don't want that to happen again."

"I don't want to hurt you, Megan. I want us to find out where this relationship can go."

"That's what I want, too, Tyler. It's the reason I wanted to be honest about my past. That may help you do the same. I want to trust you." She paused. "But you may not trust me after I tell you what I did."

What *she* did?

He cut a bite of steak, put it in his mouth, and waited. She obviously needed this time of confession.

She laid her fork on the plate, wiped her mouth with the napkin, and set it to the side of her plate. "I checked the courthouse records and then found a newspaper article about what happened with you two years ago."

What was in her eyes? Concern? Disbelief? Definitely questions.

Tyler swallowed hard, feeling as if he might choke but not from a bite of steak. His earlier instinct had been right. This was not about her after all—but him. This was what she'd been leading up to all evening. She hadn't been able to take him at face value. The awful thing was, he couldn't blame her.

She said he might not trust her? That was not the issue. "I understand. You hear things. You have to check them out."

"I feel guilty for doing that, Tyler. But when people insinuated things and said they knew something about you, I wanted to prove they were wrong."

He didn't blame her. Asking what he'd asked of her was too hard. He wished she could have waited. Given them more time. "You have no reason to feel guilty."

"The records said you were in jail for two years, Tyler. Is. . . that true?"

"Yes, it's true."

"You're. . .guilty of all those things? Stolen car? Alcohol? Drugs?"

He didn't answer immediately. He believed he was in love with Megan. But he had been out of circulation for two years. Clare, his former fiancée, had walked out on him. He had not yet completely fulfilled his debt to society. He had to think of Penny.

"I'm sorry," he said. "I'm not at liberty to talk about it yet."

"Or you won't."

The expression on her face didn't seem to be anger. Just hurt. He'd said he didn't want to hurt her, but that's what his silence was doing. No doubt in her opinion, based on the facts, he was proving to be another untrustworthy man.

Music played in the background, but it wasn't eliciting a good feeling. He'd decided long ago how he'd deal with life and relationships after prison. But this with Megan had happened so fast, and it didn't fit his plan. This was obviously not the time for a commitment. But how could he answer her?

She spoke again, quietly. "Is it true, Tyler, what the records report about you?"

He looked into her eyes. "Megan, I spent two years in prison, plus I was sentenced to 120 hours' community service at the juvenile center."

"So your teaching at the juvenile center is not a Christian service but because of a court sentence."

"Can't it be both?"

She looked around the dimly lit room then back at him. "I don't know, Tyler. You have to tell me. Now that I know, can't you explain this to me? Were you taking drugs?"

"No," he said, but he couldn't allow her to continue questioning him. He wouldn't go against what he believed was the right way to handle the situation. "Megan, I'll tell you this much. I'm on parole. My debt to society is not yet fulfilled. I have good reasons for not going into details about that. At this time I can't talk about the past."

"Can't?" Her stare challenged him. "Or won't?"

He was grateful the waitress came to refill their tea glasses. That gave him a moment to think without alienating Megan further. After the waitress left, Megan spoke in a carefully controlled tone of voice. "Tyler, I'm sorry if I haven't gone slowly enough for you. Sorry if you think I'm asking for some kind of commitment from you. If you feel you don't know me well enough to confide in me, that's fine."

"Megan, you have nothing to apologize for. I would love to have a commitment from you, and I'd like to make one. But I don't think either of us is ready for that. From what you've told me tonight, you may well be on the rebound from your fiancé's having hurt you. You are harboring hurt and anger about your family situation."

"Oh," she said, raising her eyebrows. "So this is because *I'm* not ready."

He shook his head. "No, those are simply observations we both need to face. As for me, until recently, the only women I'd spoken to in two years were Penny and Beth Templeton."

She nodded and stopped poking her vegetables and took a bite. At least she was still willing to listen to him.

"I don't think either of us is ready for a lifetime commitment." Seeing her stiffen slightly, he hurried to reassure her he was not trying to get out of their relationship. He reached across the table for her hand. "I'm falling in love with you, Megan."

Her gaze met his then. Her eyes were moist as they searched his, but she did not place her hand in his.

"Megan," he said, "I've been in love before, and so have you. A lifetime commitment takes more than just the feelings of love. I don't think either of us wants to make a mistake."

"No," she said. "I know you're right. My feelings for you grow stronger each day, Tyler. But I can't chance finding out there are things in your life I can't deal with. I need you to be honest with me. I mean. . .alcohol? Drugs? What happened? Just tell me. Do you have a problem with either?"

"No. I do not. I have never even tried drugs."

"Then why—?"

He shook his head, and she took a deep breath, closing her eyes. Obviously the questions in her mind were overwhelming. After a moment she opened her eyes and looked at him. "So for now, then," she said, "we're just. . .friends?"

"I hope so," he said.

They continued eating, even talking about the food. The waitress came and asked if they'd like dessert.

Megan smiled sweetly, looking first at the waitress, then at Tyler. Her words took on a double meaning. "I couldn't swallow another bite."

After they got into the car, Tyler turned toward Megan and put his arm over the seat, his fingers touching the soft, silky material over her warm shoulder. He spoke quietly. "Thank you for not walking out on me tonight, Megan. Clare did without even asking for an explanation. You could have, too."

She reached up and touched his fingers. He wanted to take her in his arms when he saw the tears in her eyes. "You were right about our needing to be sure, and I appreciate that. But, until you're ready to explain things to me, I think—"

He was nodding. She moved her fingers away, and he turned to start the engine. That touch on her shoulder, the feel of her fingers on his, might be the last he'd ever have from her. They were silent on the drive back to her house. He pulled into her driveway and cut the engine.

"Don't bother getting out," Megan said, opening the car door.

No, there would be no good-night kiss tonight. . .maybe never.

He watched the pain come into her eyes, or maybe it was a reflection of his own. "Tyler," she said. He knew she was about to say what he feared from the moment Clare had walked out on him. He hadn't blamed Clare. He wouldn't blame Megan. "I'll have to think about this."

He nodded, blinking away the moisture stinging his own eyes. "I know." He nodded again. "I know."

He watched her walk away. Once she paused, and he wondered if she'd turn and come back and say she would trust him. But that was too much to expect. She lowered her head as if watching her feet and then, without turning around, went inside and closed the door.

He stared at the door, then reminded himself this was no

more than he could expect. He'd known that all along.

But just as he told Penny she must get rid of the guilt, he knew he must bear that guilt as if it were his own. He'd chosen to do that, whatever the consequences.

The hard part was that he'd expected everything in his life to move slowly. Someday he'd meet a woman, and they'd fall in love, and enough time would have passed that once they became engaged he could tell her about his prison time.

Why he had met Megan on the day he was released from prison, he didn't know.

Now, again, he would live in prison, one he'd condemned himself to purposely.

He'd known that meeting a wonderful woman like Megan had been too good to be true, too soon.

Even if he told her the whole story, he would still have to deal with the problem of her friends, his friends, their acquaintances trusting him. If she knew the truth, what would she do when others made accusations against him? Where would that leave Penny? What would be the sense of the past two years?

"I knew," he said aloud, his voice faltering with emotion. "I knew." He should not have pursued. . .even slowly. . .a relationship that had nowhere to go.

He'd hurt Megan. He'd hurt himself.

He pulled out onto the road and headed for home. At least he would try to be true to his commitment to his sister and not hurt her.

fourteen

"Tyler, Dru and I are going out tonight. You and Megan want to join us?"

"One man with three women? What have I done to deserve that punishment?"

"I'll tell you," she said, placing her hands on her hips. "You've had your nose stuck in those books for a week and haven't gone out at all. Come to think of it, I don't even recall your talking with Megan on the phone. For a while you were always calling her, or she was coming by and the two of you would discuss those books or go together to see a property."

She knew his expressions and knew he was holding something back when he tried to joke. "You're monitoring my every move, mother-hen Penny?" He smiled, but his voice was serious. "I'm the older brother, remember?"

She scoffed. "Not old enough to become a recluse."

He laid his hand on his book. "You're one to talk. How often do you go out? All I see you doing is working, shopping, cleaning, cooking. As I've said before, what kind of life is that for a young woman?"

Penny feared this was turning into the kind of discussion she didn't want. But she had to try. "Tyler, I want to do things for you. You've done so much for me."

He gave her a look of warning that she was approaching a forbidden subject. And she had. He sighed. "Penny, you know you don't have to cook and clean and take care of me. Mom had a housekeeper. We can have a housekeeper. You know that. I let you do what you want, and if you want the practice of cooking dinner most nights, that's fine. But I don't expect you to do that for me."

Why can't he understand? "I want to."

He nodded. "I know you want to. But if it's part of making you feel less guilty, it hasn't worked, has it? Do you plan to take care of me for the rest of my life? Can't you accept that what I did was my choice, consequences and all, and you can't repay me? That was a gift, Penny. My gift to you. Oh, now don't start crying."

"I'm not crying. My eyes are watering. But, Tyler, are you two having problems?"

"No. Just an understanding."

"What kind?"

"Penny, that's my personal business. I'm the older brother, you know. I can handle my own life."

"Really, Tyler? And handling your life is throwing away a chance with a woman like Megan? And burying your nose in those books night after night?"

"If I'm not mistaken, that's what you do when in school. It's my future, Penny."

She moaned. "It didn't used to be. You loved teaching."

"Penny." His tone of voice was short, like a reprimand. "I love you more than I love teaching." He lifted his hands in a desperate gesture. "We don't need to get into that conversation."

"Yes, yes, we do." She frowned. "If you and Megan are having problems because of me—if she thinks you've been a terrible person, we do need to get into this. Please, Tyler, I'm a big girl now. If you have to choose between telling Megan the truth and protecting me, you have to choose her."

He shook his head. "Penny, if I told her, who would be next? Her family? A boyfriend you will someday have? Anyone who says something against me, and you think I must be defended? It has to be over, Penny. I can't go around telling things against you to a woman unless I'm sure the two of us are ready to make a commitment."

"But if she's hearing things, Tyler, that makes her think badly of you."

"Then I'll just live with that. Look at it this way. What happened two years ago is true about you. Does that make you a terrible person?" He answered before she could take a breath. "No. You're a wonderful woman who has learned from the past, who applies herself and does her best in everything she undertakes. You even go beyond the call of duty. You excel, Penny. Now if some fellow should know that and hold the past against you instead of seeing the fine person you are, then that person isn't for you."

Penny could see the reasoning in that. He always had a way of winning any debate. She'd hated that when she was a teenager and he had the control. When she looked back she saw he'd been right. She feared he was right again, but it only made her feel worse.

"I don't think I can stand it if Megan breaks up with you because of what she thinks is your past."

He nodded. "I know. It's hard for me to stand. But as I just said, any man who can't see your worth beyond a mistake you made as a teenager isn't worthy of you. In a sense it's the same here. If Megan or anyone else can't take me for the person I am, then I suppose we're not right for each other."

When he put it that way, it made sense. But it didn't make

her feel any better. If only he weren't so stubborn. She knew he cared for Megan a lot. Why didn't he just tell her the truth?

∽

The following day, as if her fight with Tyler wasn't enough, her worst nightmare walked through the front door of the inn.

Penny didn't speak, just stared and tried to show no emotion. But she'd never forgotten him. Each time she saw someone that even slightly resembled him, she felt herself tighten inside.

Sometimes when other things were going on—a party on TV, a mention of drinking, a report of an automobile accident, drugs—something would happen, and the scene that changed her life and Tyler's replayed like a rerun. Each time it evoked deep emotions.

Now Rudy walked across the marble lobby, came up, and leaned against the chest-high partition.

Penny usually remained seated when someone came in to register or ask questions, because that position was the best for acquiring housing and conference information from the computer, printing out a bill for payment, or reaching to the side for brochures. "May I help you?" she said in her most staid voice, as if he were a customer.

His eyes held a come-on look that she once had thought appealing. A half grin touched his lips. That grin no longer looked like the one on the face of that famous movie star who'd been voted "Most Attractive Man of the Year." Rudy now looked like what she knew he had been two years ago—a villain, a deceiver, a lawbreaker. How could she ever have found him attractive?

Of course she knew the answer. She'd been young and foolish, looking for the male attention she couldn't get from her deceased dad and wouldn't accept from her big brother. She'd wanted someone, anyone, to fill the void in her life. Rudy had filled it—with all the wrong things.

"Sure you can help me," he drawled, as if the smooth tone of his voice would charm her. It didn't. She felt sick. "I've been waiting for this day."

Penny could have said, "So have I." She knew she would have to confront Rudy someday. Maybe he would answer some of the questions that had plagued her.

"Why did you steal that car, Rudy?"

"I wanted to impress you. Wanted you to think I had money."

Two years ago she might have thought that a compliment. Now it sounded like a lame excuse and an insult. If that were true, which she doubted, then he hadn't thought much of her character. A stab of guilt assuaged her. Maybe she hadn't shown much back then.

"Why the drugs, Rudy?"

He shrugged. "I didn't know the drugs were in the trunk of that car."

Penny looked down, trying to hide any evidence of emotion. She didn't believe him. But if she asked how he knew drugs were in the trunk, he could say he read it in the newspaper article about Tyler's arrest.

She looked at him again. "Rudy, I was too stupid to know what was going on until later. But I've had plenty of time to think about it. I saw you giving guys little packages and them giving you money in return. When I questioned you, you said they owed you money, that they always came to you because you grew up in a wealthy family. Now I know that's not true. Someone who knew you well told me it wasn't true."

"I wanted to impress you," he said.

Whether or not that was true, she understood the concept. She'd wanted to impress him. And all it led to was trouble.

Both his elbows were now on the partition, and he leaned forward. Penny rolled her chair farther back from the desk.

The grin remained on his lips. "Let's start seeing each other again."

"Never," she said. "After what you've done?"

"Me?" He leaned back and pointed at his chest, then spread his hands. "The way I see it, your brother pled guilty to all sorts of charges. I hear he's back in town. I don't think he would want it known his little sister was drinking and driving a stolen car with drugs in it."

Her heart stopped. "What are you saying, Rudy? That you'll spread the word around that Tyler went to jail in my place? You know, it was in your place, too. We both could have reported you to the police."

His brow furrowed, and he looked like a repentant child, but she doubted his sincerity when he said, "I'm just not sure what to say to you, Penny. I've changed. I'm not the kind of guy I was back then. You're the best thing that ever happened to me, and I handled it wrong."

He gave her a lingering look that had once been effective in blocking out her common sense. "Could we see each other again? I'm not the same person, really. I wasn't raised in a good home like you. I didn't handle things well. Come on. Give me a chance to prove it."

"I'm not the same either, Rudy," she said. "I don't party anymore."

"Then how about you and me getting together? Go out with me tonight."

"I have other plans," she said and looked around him at a couple entering the lobby. "Hello. May I help you?"

Rudy moved aside, and the couple walked up to the partition.

"See ya," Rudy said and walked away.

Penny pasted on a smile and listened to the couple's requests. But she knew Rudy would be back, and she greatly feared the trouble he could bring.

❧

He came a second time. He must have waited until he saw no one else was around.

His expression and tone of voice held repentance. "You're right about me, Penny. I was a cad. And I'm not wealthy. But I've changed. If I had just a little money, I could go to college this fall. I've been living with an aunt in Hendersonville, and she says she can't keep me anymore. Do you suppose your brother would give me a loan?"

Penny could only stare. His eyebrows lifted slightly, and his lips turned into that crooked grin she'd once thought was heart-stopping. She felt her heart might stop now for an entirely different reason.

Rudy wasn't simply asking for a loan.

"Rudy, do you know what my brother would do to you if he knew you were even talking to me?"

He grinned. "I know what would happen to him if he did anything to me. He'd end up back in prison."

He turned and walked away, then looked over his shoulder and winked. She knew he'd be back for the answer.

❧

That evening she cooked a great meal, it was one of Tyler's favorites—fried chicken, creamy mashed potatoes, and steamed veggies. She hoped he'd feel sated and not be upset about Rudy's showing up.

When they'd almost finished the meal, she casually mentioned what happened. "Rudy's back."

His head came up; he stopped chewing and glared at her. Penny knew the glare wasn't about her but about Rudy. Although she blamed herself for getting into trouble, she knew Tyler blamed Rudy.

"He's not to come near you."

"I know that, Tyler. I don't want him near me. He stopped by the conference center. He apologized and said he's changed."

"Yeah, I'll bet."

"Tyler," she said as softly as she could, "*I* changed. Maybe it's true."

He shook his head. "No, Penny. Don't put yourself in the same category as Rudy. You got in with the wrong crowd and the wrong person and did some things you shouldn't have. But that wasn't your lifestyle. A guy who steals a car, tries to get a girl to drink, and has drugs in the car is different."

She nodded. "I know. But I can understand people getting into things without meaning to. Some of my friends have. I did. I was stupid. Well, other people can be stupid, too."

He closed his eyes for a moment before gazing at the ceiling, as if asking for help, then looked at her. "Are you saying you might go out with him?"

"No. Never. Even if he's a. . .a preacher now. . .I wouldn't go out with him. But, if he has changed, don't you think he could be forgiven?"

"Sure," he said shortly. "God can do things like that. But I'd like to have a face-to-face talk with that fellow. Just let me know where I can find him."

That thought was frightening. She hated having to repeat what Rudy had said. She tried to sound calm. "Tyler, you know if you find him and beat him up, you'll go back to prison."

After a long silence, he spoke in monotone. "So. This is how it is. Rudy holds our future in his hands."

"No, but let me handle this. You've said I'm a responsible woman now."

"Yes." He reached over and touched her hand. "But a very young one."

She patted his fingers. "Is just growing older what makes one wise?"

"No. It's failing and rising above it."

"Great," she said, smiling. "Then I'm qualified to handle this."

"How, may I ask?"

"I'll invite him to church." Seeing his gaze lift toward the ceiling, she spoke before he had a chance. "Tyler, I know if he comes to church that doesn't mean he's changed. I mean, I went to church all my life. I still got in with the wrong crowd. But that's a start. What he's really like is going to show, just as it did two years ago."

He pointed at her. "Now I want you to tell me anytime he comes around and anything and everything he says."

"Okay."

"Promise?" He was using his big-brother look and tone of voice.

She laid her hand over her heart. "I promise."

"All right. But remember this." He leaned over his plate. "No matter how old or how wise you become, I'll always be your big brother who loves you and tries to take care of you." His words were punctuated with a glare and taut lips.

Penny mimicked his expression and leaned over her plate. "Promise?"

She knew her response startled him for a moment, as if he'd expected an argument. Then he laughed, and she did, too. He shook his head. "You. . ."

Penny stood, walked over to him, and stopped behind his chair. Leaning against his back, she wrapped her arms around him, kissed his cheek, and then rested her cheek against his. "I love you, Tyler. I'm so glad you're my big brother. And I'm going to hold you to that promise."

His hand came up, and he held her clasped ones for a moment. She could feel the movement of his face against hers as he nodded. She knew he was emotional when he cleared his throat. But then he asked, "Now where's my dessert, woman?"

"Dessert?" She moved back, then stood beside him with her hands on her hips. "Dessert? Just what do you think I am? Your hired cook or something?"

"No way," he returned. "If I hired somebody, they'd be a better cook than this."

She tapped him on the arm. "Yeah, yeah. And who just about licked every dish clean?"

He shrugged. "Well, tonight was pretty good."

She grinned. Only people who loved each other could act like that. "Well, for that I might give you a little taste of the chocolate truffle."

"You'd better not be kidding about that," he said in a mock gruff tone.

Penny quickly turned and walked to the refrigerator to hide

the tears forming in her eyes. How could she ever come close to being as wonderful a person as her brother?

The pleasure of his love—and the pain of it—were hard to bear.

fifteen

Tyler sat on the front porch during the warm summer evening, sipping a glass of Penny's sweet tea that he liked so much. A couple of cars passed, probably men and women finishing their day of work or activity and going home to be with their families.

Megan's car was not one of them. He looked out at the lush green trees across the street and remembered how he had relished the feeling of freedom those first days out of prison.

He could thank God for the freedom just to sit on a porch with a glass of iced tea. Before prison he'd taken all that for granted and didn't always appreciate it. He warned himself now not to wish for what was not to be. He prayed that if God meant for him and Megan to have a life together, then somehow that would work out.

Mainly his thoughts were about Rudy. He feared what he might do if he confronted the boy and his attitude didn't suit him. But Penny had a point. If she'd kept on with her life the way she was heading that fateful night, she might have gone deeper into harmful activities, for herself or for others. He would have hoped and prayed she would change. Anyone deserved others to care about them and pray for them. Didn't Rudy deserve it also?

Maybe Tyler's going to prison instead of Penny had changed Rudy's life, too. Maybe Rudy had also been spared an introduction to prison life that could have made him an even more hardened criminal. Rudy might have come forward to save Penny, but Tyler could understand his not speaking up once Tyler took the blame.

After his sentencing Tyler had told his attorney the truth about the situation, but the attorney hadn't been able to find Rudy. He'd located Rudy's aunt in Hendersonville, but the boy hadn't shown up there from all they could find out. Maybe that incident scared a little sense into Rudy.

Yes, for now Tyler would do as Penny asked and trust her to be mature enough to handle this situation. She wasn't a teenager in his custody anymore. She was an adult. If she made wrong choices now, he wouldn't be responsible. He could only be there to love her.

≈

For the next two weeks Tyler studied hard, took the Realtor's exam, and passed. He considered not attending the worship service the following Sunday since there wouldn't be a sermon, but the youth were in charge with a True Love Waits program in which they would vow sexual abstinence until marriage.

But then Penny said, "Rudy came by work today. I invited him to church this Sunday. He said he would come."

That's when Tyler decided he would attend. If Rudy was going to be in the community again or around Penny, then Tyler had an obligation to talk to him. After all, Rudy was the one responsible for the events of the past two years. He prayed long and hard about it, especially that he would have the right attitude if he came face-to-face with Rudy.

He realized he wasn't angry with him except for what he'd influenced Penny to do. But Tyler believed Penny was the better for it. He was. He'd learned a lot about himself and others while in prison. He'd learned to control his tongue by seeing what happened to those who didn't. He'd learned about acceptance and getting closer to God so he could live cooped up in a cell. He'd learned about some people who were mean because they'd never had a positive influence. Some simply thought they were too smart to get caught. Some hadn't thought at all.

No, he wouldn't lose his cool with Rudy. But he did want to talk with him. To discover for himself if he thought the boy had changed or if he was toying with Penny again or trying to blackmail her. He didn't expect Rudy to tell the truth about that night two years ago and incriminate himself. Tyler didn't want that anyway. He'd taken the blame and served his sentence, and that part was over. Rudy should at least be told he didn't have to live with guilt. God would forgive him if he repented and asked. Then he could live a productive life.

Tyler arrived at the church the same time Bill did on Sunday. He left his car and started walking toward the church, when Bill caught his arm. He nodded toward a black sports car down the way.

"O you of little faith" came to Tyler's mind as he watched a young man climb out of the car.

After the young man walked on ahead of them, Bill mumbled, "I thought I recognized the broken back-up light on that car. I gave that fellow a ticket last night—not for the light, but for going sixty-eight in a forty-five-mile zone on Highway 70."

Tyler was pretty sure he knew who the guy was, but he asked Bill anyway. "Remember his name?"

Wearing a grin, Bill nodded. "Sure, since that was the only excitement of the evening. Rudolph Blackston."

When they walked inside, Tyler saw that Rudy had taken a

seat on the second row from the back on the left. "Okay if we sit here?" Tyler said.

Bill nodded, and they sat on the back row in the right section where all Tyler had to do was turn his head slightly and shift his gaze to the left to have a good view of Rudy.

Was this a direct result of his prayer? Apparently God was putting Rudy right in his path so he could observe his reactions while in church.

He felt reprimanded at another thought. God would be observing Tyler Corbin's reactions while in church.

During the singing his gaze wandered to the front of the church. The head of auburn hair with golden highlights was unmistakable. She was wearing a pale yellow dress with a matching short-sleeved jacket. He doubted she'd be wearing red with it.

After the announcements, offering, and singing, the pastor announced that the service would focus on the True Love Waits group. But before they gave their pledges, Miss Penny Corbin wanted to say a few words.

Tyler was so proud of Penny. He couldn't imagine a more beautiful Christian girl, inside and out. Her blond curls fell softly to her shoulders, and she wore a light blue summer dress. He felt she was the perfect one to introduce the program for the younger teens.

Bill poked his arm. Tyler looked at him, and Bill smiled, nodding. Tyler took that as an unspoken compliment about his sister. Rudy stared ahead, and Tyler didn't detect any discernible expression on his face. He could blend in with other young men in the church.

Penny began by saying she was older than those in the program, which consisted of high school boys and girls. "But I want to tell my story," she said, "not just of sexual abstinence, but of what playing with fire can get a person into."

Tyler's throat clenched. He knew where this was heading. He stood up. He could sense Bill staring at him.

"This is my story that really began more than two years ago."

He forgot about everyone else. "Penny, no!"

"Yes, Tyler. I have to tell it," she said, as if only the two of them were in the church. "I have to do this. . .for myself." She paused, then all but whispered, "Please."

Tyler felt Bill's tug on his sleeve then and saw heads turned in his direction. He realized Penny's need. This was not just to absolve him of wrongdoing but to absolve Penny of her guilt feelings.

His gaze moved to the left, and he saw Rudy staring at him. When their gazes met, the young man quickly turned his face away.

Tyler sat down, his head bent, his eyes focused on the floor. Had his two years spent in prison been for nothing? In vain?

His head lifted when Penny began telling of her rebellious days. She had later come to understand that, while not excusable, a lot of her actions had stemmed from her grief over losing her parents and then being thrust into the custody of her older brother whose rules she didn't like. She was seventeen then and felt she could live her life her way and was mature enough to make her own choices without Tyler telling her what to do.

He felt the impact of her words. "I have to tell this because I've prayed about it for over two years. I didn't know if I should remain silent or bring it out into the open. I haven't been sure until recently when something happened to make me see this in an even clearer sense."

Penny knew Rudy sat in a pew near the back of the church, but she focused on Tyler. "I'm telling my story because I need to," she began, "not just for my brother, but for me." Her gaze swept over the young people in the front pews. "And I want you guys to realize how easily you can mess up." She doubted any of them had someone who would take the blame for them. Even if they did, she now knew no one could escape consequences that resulted from sin.

"God forgave me that night over two years ago. But I don't think a day passed that I didn't feel the agony of it and I took back the pain. Not because God didn't forgive me but because I couldn't forgive myself."

The feeling inside was so amazing, she had to mention it. "Right now is the first time I've had complete peace about this in over two years. I need to do this. I don't have a testimony and can't be an effective witness for the Lord and my relationship with Him without telling the truth."

She left nothing out. She told of her decline after meeting Rudy. She thought she was in love with him.

She looked at the young people. "Now I know that my feelings for my boyfriend were a part of growing up, a part of human nature, but it wasn't true love. True love. . .really waits. Someone who truly loves you doesn't encourage you to give up that precious possession that should be reserved for marriage. That is not the way to prove you love someone."

Penny took a deep breath. She hadn't planned out how to tell her story and hoped she wasn't rambling. But she did know that telling her own story would be more effective than trying to preach to them about right and wrong.

"That would not prove love," she said again. "It would only

prove I chose physical feelings over my love for God and obedience to His commands. I began to drink to stifle my conscience over things I was doing and thinking about doing. I partied and told myself I was having fun.

"Then one night, I knew several of the others were not just drinking. My date was offering them something, and they were giving him money. I knew it had to be drugs. I confronted him, and he said it was harmless. No worse than drinking. When he offered me some, it was as if I saw this group and myself clearly. I didn't like it. I saw others looking at me, and I suddenly felt afraid. Like they were daring me and something terrible would befall me if they thought I wasn't part of the crowd. I'd so wanted to be part of the crowd, the girlfriend of the good-looking boy all the other girls wanted to date. I was important. I was loved. Or so I thought."

For an instant Penny's gaze met that of Beth Templeton. The woman had tears on her face, but she smiled and nodded as if approving of Penny's testimony. That gave her courage to continue.

"My date said if I tried a drug, I wouldn't be reluctant to have fun. I was just too uptight. I told him I wasn't ready for that, and he said if I wouldn't, someone else would. He went to another girl and put his arm around her, then challenged me with a look."

Penny looked at Rudy then. His eyes were wide and staring as if he were in a state of shock. Still feeling as if she had to tell the events and her feelings, she continued. "It was like I suddenly saw what it was all about. I didn't want to be like that. I didn't want a boy who would treat me with so much disrespect. I didn't want that kind of life. I was suddenly afraid, afraid of people on drugs who might not know or care what they were doing.

"I went over to the snack table and ate some chips, then poured more alcohol into my paper cup, pretending I was still part of the group. I knew my date had left the keys in the car he had driven, so when he left the room, I went out and got into the car. I had no place to go but home and hoped my brother would not be there."

Penny looked at Tyler then. He did not appear to be upset, but with his gaze on the pew ahead of him, he seemed to be listening like everyone else in the church. "Just as I turned off the main road and onto the side road leading to our house, I saw a car coming my direction. It was dark. The car slowed, and as soon as we met, I found myself staring face-to-face with my brother. In my mind he was the voice of authority that would condemn me."

She shook her head, then took a deep breath. "He was staring at me, and I was staring at him. I panicked. All I could think of was to get away. My eyes were turned to the left as I accelerated and passed him, and the car went in that direction and slammed into a tree."

Penny heard the few groans that sounded from the congregation. She had no idea what they might be thinking. But she would not stop until she'd said it all, even if they walked out on her.

"Fortunately for me the car had an airbag. Tyler was there, jerking open the door, asking if I was all right. I got out of the car and seemed to be fine. The odor of the spilled alcohol was potent. I was blubbering like an idiot."

Her audience looked sympathetic. Even the teens were listening. "I was so scared," she said. "And, to make things worse, Tyler didn't yell at me. He told me to get in his car, drive as carefully as I could, go home, then call the preacher's wife or someone else to come and make sure I was all right."

Penny shook her head again. "I told him I had messed up so bad and would take the blame. He said he had to report the accident and would take the blame for it. He said I would be arrested, and the court would be hard on me since I was underage, had been drinking, and had alcohol in the car. He would probably just get a warning, and insurance would take care of the car. I didn't know drugs were in the car and Tyler would go to jail."

She didn't bother to wipe away her tears. "Even when he knew he would go to prison, he wouldn't let me take the blame. He spent two years in prison in my place. He wanted to do that for me."

Nobody had moved until now. She saw a few heads turn slightly, and some people looked over at Tyler. His head was bent, his eyes closed.

"He's suffered enough for me, and I can no longer allow my mistakes and sins to mess up the rest of his life. I wouldn't have been able to face the terrible consequences he faced, and he knew it. Because he did that for me, I was put in the custody of Mr. and Mrs. Templeton at their request. That was the best thing that could happen to me. No one else knew the truth except them and Tyler's attorney."

She paused. "Oh, there were two others. Me and my date that night." She focused on Rudy at the back of the church. He looked frightened. He needn't be. "Incidentally, he has returned to the area recently. I got the idea he was trying to blackmail us or he'd tell the truth about my being responsible for that night. He says he's changed. And he's in church this morning. If he's sincere, maybe he would like to come up and give his testimony."

Penny saw Rudy duck his head. She'd taken it this far and knew she'd have to go further. "I'm not trying to embarrass him," she said sincerely, "but I'm simply offering him an opportunity to rid himself of guilt. I hope it wasn't blackmail he was after, but forgiveness. If he's too embarrassed to give his testimony or if he wasn't sincere about changing, I pray he will seek God's forgiveness and accept it. If not here, then somewhere."

She saw him lean forward and put his hands on the pew in front of him. He stepped into the aisle and walked out the door.

Penny swiped at her tears then. She spoke clearly despite her emotions. "I see he just left the church. I won't have to worry about blackmail now. And I hope if he wasn't sincere about having changed, he will do that and accept God's forgiveness. Living with my guilt has been almost unbearable at times."

Where she got the courage to tell all that, she didn't know. But then she realized that of course she knew. The Holy Spirit had given her the strength to speak and confess; in her own weakness, she could not have.

"Just one more thing," she said. "Tyler never wanted me to tell this. He was willing to sacrifice his reputation so I could have mine intact. What he sacrificed for me has turned me to the Lord whom I depend upon daily." She looked around at the congregation. "I think there are times when one's past can remain private. But this is not one of those times. I needed to tell you this so I can feel honest and have a truthful testimony. I am willing to face whatever consequences come from this.

I feel like. . .like I've just been released from prison."

Suddenly the congregation broke into applause, and several amens were shouted. All she could do was utter a heartfelt, "Thank you."

Through tear-blurred eyes she looked at the pastor, who came up and opened his arms to her. He hugged her, then faced the audience. "We have one fine young lady here who will touch a lot of lives with her testimony."

The congregation applauded again. When they stopped, the pastor spoke again. "Having known Tyler, I've always thought there was some kind of mistake or explanation. I think Penny has said it all and completely exonerated her brother. Tyler, is there anything you want to say?"

sixteen

Megan cried all the way through Penny's testimony. She felt so ashamed of not having trusted Tyler. He was the most noble person she'd ever known. She couldn't imagine ever being good enough for him.

After Penny's confession Megan watched Tyler go up on the stage. He explained that he had never wanted Penny's story known. He didn't know if he had been right or wrong. But he'd never been so proud of his sister as he was this day. He put his arm around her shoulders and drew her near. Pride was etched all over his face. Penny's expression of love as she lifted her tearstained face to look at him was beautiful to behold.

Tyler glanced down at her, then smiled at the congregation. "My sister is a brave, wonderful young woman, thanks to the Templetons, the missionary couple she stayed with while I was away, and thanks to you in this church who embraced her. You have my respect and gratitude."

The congregation broke into applause. Then they stood. Tyler and Penny walked down and sat on the front row. When everyone else sat, the preacher said, "Now *that's* church."

He cleared his throat, but his words were tinged with emotion. "It's a better example of Christian love in action than I could ever present in a sermon. It's an example, on a much lower scale, of what Jesus did for us when He took our punishment. Penny has punished herself through the inability to forgive herself. She has suffered the consequences, although God forgave her and her brother took her punishment. But she still had to suffer the consequences of guilt for herself and the effect her actions had on other people. We've just seen an example of the biblical kind of love described by Jesus when He said, 'Greater love has no one than this, that he lay down his life for his friends.' Friends include brothers, sisters, parents, children. I'm not trying to make Tyler out as some superhero. As he said, he didn't know if he was right or wrong, but he knows great good has come from this."

The youth pastor kept the rest of the service brief. The young people agreed they needed to regroup and discuss Penny's testimony and return another time for their True Love Waits service. She had given them much food for thought.

After the service, church members crowded around Penny and Tyler. Megan turned to Libby. "I can't go out to eat today."

Libby understood. "You want the two of us to go somewhere and talk?"

"Thanks, but I don't think I can even talk."

When Megan returned home, she had a call from her aunt Eva who said she'd be eating out with friends. Megan lay in a lounge chair on the patio, alternating sipping sweet tea and wiping away the tears that just wouldn't stop. She'd messed up so miserably. She'd had a chance with the most wonderful man in the world but hadn't trusted him, hadn't taken him at face value as he'd asked.

The emotion was exhausting, and she dozed beneath the shade of the awning. When Aunt Eva came home, Megan said she couldn't talk about it, and then it all poured out. So did the tears.

Aunt Eva listened without comment until Megan had told what she could remember.

"Are you finished?" Aunt Eva asked after a moment of silence.

"Yes." Megan sniffed and raised the tissue to her nose. "Definitely finished. He will want to have nothing to do with me—ever."

"Is that what he said?"

Megan thought a moment. "No. I was the one who decided to think about our relationship. I couldn't trust him."

Aunt Eva leaned over from her chair and touched Megan's arm. "Honey, do you think he loves you?"

"He said— " She hiccupped, then sniffed. "He said—he thought he was falling in love with me, but neither of us was ready to make a commitment."

"You think he's right?"

"Oh, yes."

"That's not what I meant, Megan." Aunt Eva spoke in a soft voice. "If you've finished wallowing in the slough of despond, let's analyze this."

Megan doubted she was finished. She'd likely be wallowing for a long time.

"He's a rare kind of man who loved his sister enough to spend two years in prison in her place," Aunt Eva said. "Right?"

Megan nodded.

"But he can turn off and on his love for a woman. Is that what you're saying?"

"Well, he didn't say he loved me. He said he thought he was falling."

"Then why would he have stopped falling?"

"Because—because I rejected him."

"Rejected what?"

"Trusting him. Taking him at face value."

"He sounds like a smart man. Don't you think he understands why you couldn't do that?"

"I don't know."

"Sure you do. The only thing that has changed is you no longer have to take him at face value. You know his past and why he wouldn't talk about it. He was protecting his sister's reputation. You've changed, Megan. Not him."

Shaking her head, Megan admitted, "I feel like I'm not good enough for him."

"Okay, so how do you become good enough? Oh, I know. The next time someone commits a crime, volunteer to take their punishment for them."

That made Megan laugh. "I don't think so."

Aunt Eva's tone turned more serious. "Megan, you said he didn't even know if he did the right thing. He's not putting himself up as some hero or superhuman. And haven't you heard the saying that a woman chases a man until he catches her?

"I've heard that saying all kinds of ways."

"Oh. Well, the point is, he pursued you. Now you let him know you want to be pursued."

"It's too late. I had my chance and messed it up."

Aunt Eva stood. "When all else fails, pray." She marched across the patio and into the house.

Now there *is wisdom.* Megan asked herself why she hadn't thought of praying earlier, instead of as a last resort.

૨ક

Tyler would like to have invited Megan out, but the fact remained he hadn't trusted her with the truth. The problem between them wasn't what the truth turned out to be but that he had hidden it from her.

To her, that would appear to be a lack of trust on his part, which in turn would cause her to mistrust him.

Pastor Wrend invited Penny and Tyler home for beef stew his wife had put in the slow cooker that morning.

They went, not wanting to be out in public where people who knew them would stop and talk. Tyler didn't want to be treated as some kind of hero, or idiot, whatever the case. Neither did Penny.

Tyler and the pastor sat at the kitchen table while his wife put rolls in the oven to warm. Penny, who had eaten there many times with the Templetons, set the table.

Pastor Wrend praised them for what they'd done.

Tyler said, "I think I did the right thing, but I'm not sure. Penny was raised in the church and gave her heart to Jesus at a young age. A lot of teens go the wrong way for a while and then return to the Lord. I believe she would have done that."

Penny arranged the silverware beside his plate. "I think you're partly right, Tyler. Even in my worst moments, I could not escape God. He was always with me, correcting yet loving."

"You know, Tyler," the pastor said, "this story might be good for those boys you teach at the juvenile center. I'm sure it had an impact on the youth at church."

Tyler looked at Penny for her reaction.

"Oh," Penny said, "that's a great idea. Pastor Wrend, you've preached that some good comes from everything if we trust in the Lord. If my story could help those boys—"

Smiling, the pastor interrupted. "That, my dear Penny, would be good."

❧

Tyler was glad he could be honest with the boys at the juvenile center. Being able to tell them what Penny had learned might have more of an impact than his teaching what the Bible had to say about right and wrong. And he didn't know how some of the guys he'd been in prison with had turned out. He had seen firsthand that Penny had been heading in the wrong direction and had made a 180-degree turn. And now she was a shining example of a young woman trying to live her life the way Jesus wanted her to.

So Tyler told the story, simply and carefully.

"You really did that?" Hulk questioned, looking doubtful.

"Yes. I couldn't bear to think of my seventeen-year-old sister being in jail."

Hulk gave a short laugh. "Wish somebody would do that for me."

"Somebody did more than that for you," Tyler said.

That gave him the opportunity to talk about what Jesus did, trying to be careful not to give the impression he was on the same level with Jesus. "But I want to make it clear. I'm not sure I was right in taking my sister's punishment. It turned out well. But for the most part we each have to suffer the consequences of our actions."

He looked around. Some were looking at him like he was some kind of idiot. A boy named Jim, who always seemed receptive to his teacher, nodded. Apparently he understood the analogy. He raised his hand.

"You have a question, Jim?"

"Do you think your sister might come and tell us her story?"

"I think she would," Tyler said. He didn't want it to seem as if he were committing Penny to do it. She might not feel comfortable speaking to the young boys. "She's busy working and taking care of our home and will return to college soon. But I'll ask."

Hulk stared at him as if he'd completely lost his mind.

"I hope you don't think less of me because I gave the impression I had committed those crimes. The prison experience is the same, regardless of how I got there. The situation is still something you guys need to avoid at all costs. I didn't tell the whole story because I thought it would negate what I'd done for her. I didn't want it to look like I was trying to be some kind of hero. I was just trying to do what I thought best for her."

"Man, I'd never do that," Hulk said. Some of his followers nodded and laughed, giving sly glances to each other.

After the session ended and the boys were leaving the classroom, Tyler put his materials in his briefcase, snapped it shut, and looked up to see the bully sitting at the back of the room.

He braced himself for whatever might happen with Hulk. He'd heard the foul language and knew a lot of young people, especially troubled ones, could explode at a moment's notice. Most of the time things were orderly, but some violent acts had taken place at the center.

The boy stood when Tyler approached him. "I meant it when I said I wouldn't do that. Here I have to act like I'm tough." He grinned and ducked his head in a way that made Tyler realize he was just a kid, no matter how big his body. The boy glanced at the doorway lest someone else hear him. "I have to act that way, or somebody will beat me up. But what you said is the first time it ever made sense about what Jesus did. I never believed that"—he cleared his throat, and instead of saying whatever was on the tip of his tongue said—"stuff."

The boy shifted his weight from one foot to the other. "I didn't really try to understand it. I'm not supposed to listen to teachers, especially when they talk religion. I wouldn't tell anyone else this, but I don't ever want to come back here or go to prison. I only have a couple of more weeks before I'm free. Maybe someday I could come back and talk to guys like you do. Most of the time I think nobody cares about us. But I think you really do."

Tyler nodded. "I do. I don't want to see anyone waste their lives. Places like this can help, but it's mainly punishment for a crime committed. If you don't have a commitment to Jesus Christ, though, then you don't have a real reason on the outside to do more than try to satisfy yourself. That leads to trouble."

The boy cleared his throat again. "Can you. . .will you. . .tell me how to. . .commit to Jesus Christ?"

Tyler felt something wash over him like an ocean wave. The bad guy wanted Jesus in his heart. God kept answering prayer. Whether Tyler had done right or wrong, God continued to bring good out of the situation.

The classroom doors at the center were never to be closed, particularly with an outsider and an inmate. But Tyler closed the door. It would be all right. That wooden door didn't matter. The important door was the one to Hulk's heart, upon which Jesus was knocking.

seventeen

Where there had been rumors and insinuations before, now people discussed Tyler openly. Everyone Megan knew talked about him. They all agreed he was a rare kind of man.

In the office Ted admitted he'd had some harsh thoughts about Tyler and was glad he was wrong. "Megan, you're the one who finally got through to me about letting God be in my life. Well, now you're not setting too good an example by not going to Tyler and telling him how you feel."

She sighed and looked away.

But Ted hadn't finished lecturing her. "Megan, when I'm wrong, I say it. And you should do the same. Tyler's a smart guy. He understands your motives in not trusting him. I do, and I'm not even as close to you as Tyler has been. You have a problem with trust. Go talk to him. Tell him."

Her friends were telling her the same thing. Everyone finally talked her into it. Now she was praying about it. If Tyler wasn't God's choice for her, then things wouldn't work out for them to be together. But suppose it turned out as wonderfully as it had for him and Penny. He was reunited with his friends, his church. She knew he wasn't the kind of person to come to her and say he wasn't so bad after all and ask her to go out with him. No, she'd been the one to say she had to think about their relationship. Now this was something she had to do, no matter what the results. They had been close. She needed to let him know she respected and admired him.

On Friday after work Megan called Tyler's home number.
A woman answered.

"Penny?" She knew it wasn't Penny's voice.

"No, this is Clare Shipley. Penny isn't here. Could I take a message?"

"No. No message. Thank you."

Megan hung up. That put things into perspective. Now that everything was out in the open, Tyler and Clare could get back together. No wonder Tyler had wanted to take things slow. He wasn't over Clare. And apparently Clare wasn't over him. At least, Clare could tell him some unknown caller had asked for Penny but left no message.

The message for Megan was loud and clear.

❧

Tyler was heading for the front porch with a pitcher of iced tea and two glasses when the phone rang. He would have let the answering machine pick up, but Clare wanted to do even the smallest thing for him to make up for her attitude in the past. She had come to apologize for not even asking for an explanation after he was arrested. He kept telling her he didn't blame her for walking out on him. She'd gone on with her life and was seriously involved with someone else, but she felt she had to apologize.

"Want me to get that?" she asked.

"Sure," he said, wondering if that might be yet another caller expressing appreciation for what he'd done for his sister and for Penny's bravery in confessing. In this town, news traveled fast.

Clare picked up the phone.

Tyler heard her side of the conversation and assumed it was for Penny. Later, however, after Clare left, he checked the caller ID. Megan had called. He returned the call, but her answering machine picked up so he left a message.

≈

On Sunday, at Hulk's request, Tyler drove to Hendersonville to talk with the boy's parents. He told them about the change in their son, and at first they were doubtful. By the time he left, however, they seemed receptive to what he had to say and even said they would start attending church and learn more about this faith that changed people's hearts.

Tyler thanked God on the drive home for the good that was coming from his and Penny's experiences.

When he returned home and checked his phone messages, he discovered Megan had not returned his call. He longed to see her, and early Monday morning he stopped by the real estate agency.

For the first time, Ted greeted him enthusiastically and came forward to shake his hand. "Good to see you, Tyler. How're things?"

"Good," Tyler said, although his feelings didn't match his words. He walked over to Megan's desk.

"Hi," she said rather coolly. Her gaze didn't quite lock with his even when she asked, "Can I help you?"

"I, um, noticed you called Friday. Were you. . .calling for Penny?" Suddenly he realized she might really have called to talk with Penny, to tell her she appreciated her testimony. He was walking that fine line between being a hero and an idiot.

"No." She looked up at him then. Briefly. "I called you."

He smiled at her although her gaze skittered all around him. "Could we go out to lunch and talk about why you called?"

She glanced at Ted, who apparently had become all ears. "Go on," Ted said. "It's almost lunchtime, and I have things covered here."

Tyler didn't know if her stare at Ted meant "Thanks" or "Stay out of it."

But she said, "Okay," opened a bottom desk drawer, and took out her purse. She adjusted the purse strap over her shoulder and walked around the desk. "I'll see you later," she told Ted.

"Take your time," he replied.

While walking across the street and up the back steps to the Veranda, Tyler didn't attempt small talk. He wasn't sure if he should apologize for putting her through a difficult time or simply wait for her to mention why she called.

He waited.

After easy camaraderie with the proprietor, Jeff, and the waitress at the restaurant, Megan unfolded her napkin, placed it on her lap, then looked across at him. "The reason I called, Tyler, was to say I'm proud of you and Penny."

"Thank you."

"And I'm sorry I couldn't do as you asked and take you at face value."

"No, no." He didn't want her to feel that way. "I understand. I had no right to ask such a thing. How many women do you think would even say they needed to think about it?"

She shrugged.

"One in a million." He added, "Maybe."

She smiled faintly. "I wish I could have been that one in a million."

"No," he said. "That wouldn't have been wise. You might have agreed to trust a drug pusher."

He thought his point was well taken. "I didn't want to lose you, Megan. But I couldn't give the details of my prison time unless I was sure you and I were ready for a lifetime commitment."

The waitress brought their food and set their bowls of soup and house rolls in front of them. Tyler laid his hands, palms up, on the table. Megan placed her hands in his. He asked the blessing. When he didn't release her hands right away, she didn't pull away.

After a moment she withdrew her hands and picked up her spoon, then met his gaze. "Are you seeing Clare again?"

"No," he said, and Megan glanced at him. He thought he saw a glimmer of delight in that glance.

He decided it was time he was honest with himself and Megan about Clare. "At one point I thought we were headed for marriage," he said. "We were compatible, both teachers, attracted to each other. We became good friends and enjoyed each other's company. I think we loved each other. But we were not in love."

"Did you discover that when you saw her again?"

"No," he said. "I had a lot of time to think while in prison. I suspected it then, and I'm certain now. Seeing her again confirmed it. It's a good thing to find out you're not right for each other, but it shouldn't mean you can't be cordial with each other."

Megan agreed. "I have a couple of weeks of vacation coming up, so I'm going to Charlotte and do just that. Penny's testimony made me realize what I have to do and what you hinted at several times. I have to face my past, too."

Tyler nodded. Yes, that would be another good that came from what had happened. Everything had a ripple effect like a stone tossed into a pond. One's actions affected not just oneself, but a lot of people.

Okay, so she would face her past. But what would it mean? Did she need to find out if Tyler was the man for her? That her ex-fiancé was? What if she decided neither of them was right for her?

❧

Megan didn't see Tyler again before she left for Charlotte. Friday evening after work she made the long drive to her mom's and felt a sense of nostalgia in the room that had been hers years before. The décor had changed, but it still elicited memories, bad and good.

On Sunday Megan attended church alone. Her mom had stopped going regularly after her husband had the affair and left the family. She said it was too humiliating. She hadn't minded if Megan and her sister, Janet, went. Janet chose not to very often. Megan had found the faith preached at church was a comfort in believing Jesus loved her.

Her mom's excuse this Sunday was that Janet and the children were coming for supper. She wanted to make sure everything was right. "I've been going more often lately," her mom said. "I see George there sometimes. He's asked about you." Her eyes brightened. "Maybe you'll see him there."

"Maybe," Megan said.

Megan sat on the third pew from the back. She noticed George sitting midway on the right side of the aisle. Since his arm was across the back of the pew where a woman sat, she could only assume they were together. Yes, just seeing him again confirmed a lot of things in her mind.

After the service her glance met George's surprised one. Not wanting to speak to him, she hurried toward the exit.

She was welcomed warmly by a few people at the back who recognized her.

That afternoon she and Janet were on the patio watching the children play and catching up on each other's lives when their mom came out with the phone.

"For me?" Megan asked.

Her mom nodded, and Megan reached for the phone. "Oh, hi, George." She deliberately said his name to intrigue her mom and sister, who stared at her with lifted eyebrows and wide eyes.

"Yes, I saw you at church. No, I'm not back to stay. Just visiting." He then said he thought if she were going to be there awhile they might get together and talk about old times. The woman with him at church was just a friend. Nothing serious.

Megan had heard that line before when she'd confronted him about his having been seen with another woman. He'd admitted it, saying they were friends. But she had learned he was seeing this "friend" frequently. He'd said she was Rena, a neighbor he'd known for many years, and the two had become closer after her divorce.

Megan had decided to check out the diner she'd heard they frequented. She saw firsthand how friendly they were, sitting on the same side in a booth, their bodies close and their lips together—and not in a kiss she'd call just "friendly." She'd lost her cool and told him off. The worst part was that Rena simply sat there smiling.

He called later that night and apologized profusely, saying neither of them meant for that to happen. But Megan remembered that when she left the diner George hadn't come after her. He'd stayed with Rena.

Soon after that Megan went to live with Aunt Eva.

In her imagination George would follow her and say he made a mistake, but she would laugh and say he would have to live with it. She would gloat.

But now that she'd seen George again, she didn't want to gloat. The woman with him at church was not Rena. Now he was saying this woman was "just a friend." She listened as he told her how good it was to see her again and complimented her on her looks.

"Thanks, George. I'm glad you called. I've wanted to say I'm sorry our last meeting was so heated. I was angry and hurt and emotional. I'm not angry anymore."

That must have sounded like an invitation to him. He immediately said, "Could we get together while you're here?"

"There's no need for that, George. We really don't have anything to talk about. I wish you every happiness."

There was silence. "You, too," he finally managed to say.

They said good-bye, and she pushed the button that broke the connection. That action felt like closing a book she had no desire to open again.

৯

"I'm going to forgive him," Megan said. She and her mother and sister were enjoying a cup of coffee after the supper dishes were loaded in the dishwasher and her sister's children were outside playing.

"Who?" Janet asked, lowering her cup. "George or Dad?"

"Good question," their mother said, setting her cup on the table. "We were discussing George until Janet said your dad and Brenda took the kids to a movie yesterday."

Megan recognized the stiff look on her mom's face at the mention of her father's second wife.

"Oh, sorry. I was still thinking about George. But—"

Megan feared adding what came to mind. For the past several years every time the family got together it became a Dad-bashing time. Emotions ran high, and often other arguments ensued because everyone was on edge. That was another reason Megan had wanted to leave Charlotte. Dealing with George's unfaithfulness and her parents' nasty divorce had been too much.

She dared say what she thought. "I'm going to do my best to forgive Dad, too."

Janet's cup hit the table hard. "What? After all he's put this family through, you're going to take his side?"

Megan saw the glare in Janet's eyes and the lowering of her mother's gaze to her cup. If she could keep her voice at an even keel, maybe her mom and Janet would see her point. Each one yelling their opinions had never accomplished anything.

She would try. "That doesn't mean I think Dad was right. And it's not taking sides. He has to answer for his actions, just like Mom does. Like me and George. My hard feelings toward George harmed only me. Trying to punish Dad by rejecting him is hurting me. I don't want to do that to myself anymore."

Janet's glare had not softened. Megan figured the only reason she wasn't yelling was because she was too shocked. Their mom was playing with the handle of her cup and didn't look too happy.

"I know the hurt Dad has put us through. I know Mom has suffered, because I have about George, but it isn't nearly as bad as if we'd been married."

"I can't believe this!" Janet half rose from her chair.

"Wait, Janet," Mom said, holding out her hand as if to stop her. "Megan's right."

Janet slid back into her chair, her mouth open and her eyes staring at her mom.

"All my anger and hurt haven't changed the situation with your dad one bit."

Janet shook her head. "Well, you had every right to be hurt." She pointed from herself to Megan. "So did we. And his grandchildren. Now they go to the movies with Dad and his office manager."

Their mother spoke quietly. "She's his wife."

"Well. . ." Janet was dumbfounded. "That isn't right."

Megan was not surprised her mother agreed. None of them could say his actions had been right. "Yes, but I need to forgive him, too," she said. "As Megan said, I'm hurting myself. I've wanted to punish him and felt good about you girls taking my side in this."

Megan felt for her, and Janet reached over and touched her when she wiped away a tear. "But I've watched you girls talk against your dad, and that's not right either. He didn't deliberately hurt you. And I know he loves you. We all need to forgive him, for our own sakes."

Janet looked at her mom steadily, but she didn't yell. "That may take awhile."

Her mom nodded. "That's all right. I don't know if I ever will completely. But I don't want to harbor anger and resentment anymore. I need to get on with my life."

They each had tears on their faces now, but they reached across and held each other's hands. Megan knew it was her mother who had lost her husband. That didn't mean she had to lose her dad. She called him that night and asked if they might have lunch together the next day. He said yes.

Megan felt proud of herself when she said, "It's okay if you want to bring Brenda."

૨**ə**

Outside the restaurant Megan waited in her car until her dad and Brenda drove up. When she stepped out of the car, she saw the uncertainty on their faces. But when she smiled, her dad opened his arms, and Megan fell into them.

She had missed that. She needed her dad. The way he held her and said her name made her feel as if he needed her, too.

eighteen

"No, I haven't seen Rudy again," Penny told Tyler. "I don't know if he was embarrassed that Sunday when I asked him to give his testimony or if he hasn't really changed. I suspect the latter since he hasn't shown up again at the conference center."

"It's just as well, Penny," Tyler said, trying not to show his relief.

"What about you and Megan? How do things stand now?" Tyler confided in her.

"Do you think she'll come back from Charlotte?" she asked.

"We agreed to pray about our relationship. We've both learned the hard way something all young people need to learn. Love isn't just feelings or physical attraction. It's a willingness to spend a lifetime to make a relationship work. We're feeling our way through right now."

His sister could probably detect a sadness in his words, but he was not one to mope. He had taken a part-time job with a real estate firm in Asheville and continued to teach at the juvenile center in the mornings.

"You must feel as if a huge burden has been lifted from you, Penny. I'm so proud of you for what you did." He wanted to take the focus off his own circumstances.

"I do, Tyler, and I can never repay you for what you did—and I know you don't want me to try. But I needed to tell the truth for my own sake.

"Everyone thinks you're a terrific hero, and I expected that."

Penny smiled. "What I'm really surprised about, though, is that they seem to think I did something wonderful by confessing my sinful past. Not the bad stuff I did, of course, but telling the truth in front of everybody."

Tyler waited for her to go on.

"It was hard, but not nearly as hard as keeping it inside. And now no one seems to hold my past against me—not that I can tell anyway. All my friends have gone out of their way to support me, and some have even told me about stuff they've done in the past."

"I guess you can say more good has come out of it," Tyler said.

Penny nodded thoughtfully.

❧

A few days later he drove Penny to the juvenile center so she could talk with the boys. He listened as she told them how easy it was to get on the wrong road, but how rewarding to start over, to give one's life to the Lord and do something worthwhile by seeking God's will.

Tyler noticed they all seemed to listen. He had told her on the way out to expect some sneers or mumbles. But instead the boys applauded when she finished, and afterward Tyler heard several come up to thank her.

They rode in silence for a little while. Then Penny spoke. "I'll never be grateful for messing up and causing you to go to prison, Tyler. But, like you, I can see the good that's come from it." She sighed.

Tyler smiled. Even though the relationship with Megan wasn't going the way he'd hoped, at least Penny was on the right track. She had a testimony that would help others make the right choices.

"You know what, Tyler?" Penny turned to him. "I'm going to try to speak to youth groups at churches and maybe at schools, too." She hesitated. "I never told you this, but in the past two years, acquaintances have offered me alcohol and drugs. They always implied I was a Goody Two-shoes for refusing." She smiled. "But now I can say, 'Let me tell you why I refuse.'"

Tyler reached over and squeezed his sister's hand, grateful to the Lord for what He had done.

❧

"Tyler, are you sure you don't want me to come home this weekend?" Penny said over the phone. "Aren't you lonely without me?"

"Sure. I'm real lonely at suppertime when I have to cook my own food."

"Seriously, Ty. Tell me the truth."

"Of course I miss you, little sis. But I want you to stay on campus and mingle with young people your own age anytime you want to."

"Well, several of us are working on things for the Christian student union, and a concert is coming up this weekend. Shauna and I were talking about going."

"Perfect. Enjoy yourself."

"I love you," they both said before hanging up.

Tyler looked around. He did miss Penny. He missed Megan. He missed his parents. But after having been restricted to a prison and enclosed in an eight-by-eight-foot cell behind bars every night, he had learned to turn everything over to the Lord. That and keeping busy made all the difference.

He was glad Penny was involved at Western and wouldn't be home for the weekend. He was glad she no longer felt she had to take care of him. Confessing her past had taken away her guilt in a way that serving him had not been able to do.

She'd learned a valuable lesson. No one could work hard or long enough to rid themselves of guilt. A person could only confess it, repent of it, and allow the Holy Spirit to fill that life. Penny was a wonderful example of having done that.

He needed to be an example of a man who could function even when he didn't get everything he wanted. Part of that would be to devote more attention to his job.

On Friday at work he received an e-mail from Ted, saying he had a client interested in seeing the Sunrise Mountain property Tyler had listed. Ted couldn't get away on Saturday and wondered if Tyler would show it to his client. Could he meet at 10:00 a.m. on Saturday?

Tyler figured that meant Megan hadn't returned and maybe never would.

Normally Tyler didn't go to the office or show property on Saturday. But an occasional veering from his schedule was all right.

He left home shortly before 9:15 a.m. to give him plenty of time in case he was caught in traffic. The August sun was already shining brightly. There wasn't much traffic since school had started in most areas, which meant many tourists had returned to their homes in other states.

He turned off the interstate and wound up and around the mountain. As soon as he turned onto the property he was overcome by the view—not just the scenery of mountain peaks spread out beyond nor the closer lush foliage of trees. Lovely Megan stood near her red car, looking out over the panoramic scene.

After letting out a deep breath, he walked near and spoke as calmly as he could. "Good morning, ma'am. I understand you're interested in this property."

Standing behind her, he watched her shoulders lift slightly. "When I read on the Internet that you'd listed this, I came up and looked. . . . No, not really."

She turned toward him then, and he saw her tear-filled eyes.

"What I said was true. But my reason for asking you here was because I wanted to see you privately. To apologize." She raised her hand, and he saw she held a red rose. "You said no one ever gave you roses. I wanted to give you this. Oh, Tyler, you deserve more than one rose. It's just a token—"

Elated at what this might mean but trying to be cautious, he joked, "Then where are the other eleven? Surely a dozen—" He stopped abruptly when she tried to laugh, but a tear slid down her cheek.

He lifted his hand and gently brushed away the tear with his thumb. "I'm trying to joke, Megan, but I should let you say what you came here to say."

They walked along the crest of the ridge while she thanked him for knowing she needed to get the past settled. She told of seeing George and her dad and the good results from both. She let go of her hurt and resentment. She could even thank God she hadn't married George.

Tyler ventured to ask, with hope in his heart, "Why is that?"

"Because," she said with a catch in her voice, "because I know I can live without someone, even someone I thought I loved. I learned that life doesn't stop when you're disappointed in another person. There is still so much life out there, so many challenges, others you can love. So. . .thank you."

"You're welcome, Megan. I know what you mean. I learned that, too, when I saw Clare again. Sometimes we can leave a situation and go on. Other times we need some kind of closure. I think both you and I needed that."

She nodded. "Like Penny needed closure, too. And that brings me to my apology. I'm so sorry I didn't trust what I believed you to be. I judged you as if you weren't good enough for me when it's the other way around."

He caught hold of her arm then and turned her toward him. "That's so far from the truth. I'm not even sure that what I did was right. I believed it was better for me to go to prison than for Penny to go to some kind of institution. But whether it's right to take another's punishment for their wrongs, I don't know."

"Good came from it," she said. "Except you may not be able to teach in a public school again."

"That's all right," he said. "I can teach at the juvenile center. Perhaps make a bigger difference there. I don't know. I like teaching in the public school system, and if that's God will for my life, then it will work out. If not, I'm open to possibilities."

"Oh, Tyler, just say you forgive me."

"Of course I forgive you," he said. "And I know a way to make you feel better. You can marry me and find out I have a lot of faults. Then you'll feel like a saint."

The look on her face relaxed, and a light came into her eyes. She backed up and leaned against a tree. A small grin touched her lips. "If that's a proposal, the answer is yes."

He came close and propped his hand behind her shoulder. Mingled with the aroma of lush foliage in bloom was the faint fragrance of a tantalizing perfume. Even more tantalizing was the nearness of her. "That wasn't a complete proposal," he said, stepping in closer and fixing her gaze with his. "I want you to pick out an engagement ring. I'll plan something elaborate and get on my knees to propose."

She whispered, her lips close to his. "This is just a sample of how I will respond." Their lips met, and his arms encircled her waist. She reached up and put hers around his neck.

When their commitment was sealed, Tyler pulled away. "If that's just a sample, I suggest we tie the knot quite soon."

Megan laughed and agreed.

nineteen

Megan stood in a side room with her wedding attendants, trying her best to be calm. At least there had been no family tension in the preceding weeks and months while plans were made and showers given. Her mom said it was time she forgave her husband, as Megan had forgiven George. She hadn't resisted when Megan suggested that Brenda also sit with the family since she was the wife of Megan's dad.

Tyler had chosen John Templeton as his best man, and they agreed Beth would be seated as mother of the groom.

The door opened enough for Vera to peek in. She attended the church and helped plan most of the weddings held there. "It's almost time," she said.

Almost time.

Megan felt that she shouldn't be thinking of George at a time like this. But there he was, in her mind. It now seemed a lifetime ago she thought she would be walking down the aisle to him. That thought now made her shiver. How close she had come to making the biggest mistake of her life.

She remembered Tyler had said he had loved Clare but hadn't been in love with her. He had said when you love someone it's reasonable, understandable. When you're in love, it's in spite of yourself, in spite of reason.

Megan smiled, thinking about that. She loved Tyler for all his wonderful qualities. But she had loved him unreasonably when she doubted and questioned those qualities. Her feelings for him far surpassed those she'd had for George.

The door opened wide. Vera said they could go into the foyer. While organ music filled the air and family members were escorted to their seats, Megan held her shaking hands together and visualized the sanctuary. She and Tyler had chosen to be married on a Friday evening, two weeks before Christmas to take advantage of the lovely church decorations. A huge, green wreath made from balsam fir hung high over the choir loft. White lights intermingled with red poinsettia leaves. On each side of the dais stood two tall balsam firs softly lit in white.

Red poinsettias adorned the partition separating the choir loft from the dais. During church and the wedding rehearsal, Megan had formed a mental picture of her wedding day. But she had not experienced such anxiety until now.

Bill Probe had been delighted and surprised when Tyler asked him to serve as a groomsman. He looked quite handsome in his black tux and bowtie. He held out his arm for Libby, and the two began to make their way down the center aisle.

Libby, Kay, and Penny looked beautiful in their red satin dresses with white sashes, carrying bouquets of red roses. Tyler and a teacher named Chad had resumed their former friendship. Chad escorted Kay down the aisle. Another friend, Marshall, who was Tyler's best friend in college and had visited him in prison, escorted Penny.

Megan took a deep breath while Janet, her matron of honor, gave last-minute instructions to her son and daughter, the ring bearer and flower girl. Then Janet graciously strolled down the aisle.

"I have to look," Megan whispered to Vera and her dad. She

stood at the side of the entry and peeked around. After Janet reached the front, Vera gently urged the children forward.

Pleased sounds of laughter came from the onlookers when Janet's daughter, Missy, stopped to rearrange an errant rose petal.

Feeling a tap on the shoulder of her white satin gown, Megan straightened and walked over to her dad, who smiled encouragingly at her and offered his arm.

Vera straightened the train of her dress and made sure her veil hung perfectly. The wedding march began, and everyone stood, turned, and watched the door.

Megan hardly saw them now, and she had no idea if her steps were slow or in time with the music.

Her gaze moved to Pastor Wrend standing in a white robe, holding a Bible. On the left were her matron of honor and bridesmaids. On the right were Tyler, his best man, and the groomsmen.

Tyler looked so handsome in his black tux, white satin cummerbund, and rosebud boutonniere. But more important was that his gaze did not move from her. Why didn't they let brides run down the aisle to the man they loved, instead of going at a snail's pace?

She hadn't seen such a look of pleasure on his face since the day she said she'd marry him. In only a few minutes that would happen. She was about to begin the rest of her life with the man she loved.

As she reached the front of the church, Tyler stepped down and stood beside her. She kept looking at him, and he at her. She couldn't stop smiling at him as they exchanged their vows and the rings. Then it happened. They were pronounced, legally and under God, man and wife.

Later, on the way to Tyler's home where they would spend the night, snow began to fall. "A perfect ending to a wedding," Megan said, delighted.

"A perfect beginning for a marriage," Tyler said. "But this time tomorrow we'll be experiencing the sunshine of Hawaii."

"Are you sure the sun will be shining?"

"Positive. If the roads are icy and we're snowed in, no problem." He looked over at her. "Wherever you are, the sun will be shining." He put his hand over his heart. "Right here."

"Ohh." She smiled. "How sweet."

She looked out at the soft snow covering the ground like a blanket. Tyler drove carefully through it. "I can't help but wonder, Tyler, how this might have turned out if Penny hadn't told the truth."

"I think all this would have been delayed." He carefully maneuvered the car up the driveway and into the garage. He switched off the engine and the lights and then turned to her as the garage door lowered. "I know I wouldn't have stopped loving you."

"Nor I you," she said.

"Carrying you over the threshold will have to wait," he said, his fingers drawing a path along her cheek. "There's something I want to do right now, Mrs. Corbin."

"I love the sound of that," Megan said softly, leaning toward him.

He traced a pattern over her lips with his finger. "I love you."

"I love you," she whispered against his lips.

After the kiss Megan touched his face. The kiss had been sweet and slow. No need to hurry. They had a lifetime together.

A Letter To Our Readers

Dear Reader:
In order that we might better contribute to your reading enjoyment, we would appreciate your taking a few minutes to respond to the following questions. We welcome your comments and read each form and letter we receive. When completed, please return to the following:

Fiction Editor
Heartsong Presents
PO Box 719
Uhrichsville, Ohio 44683

1. Did you enjoy reading *By Love Acquitted* by Yvonne Lehman?
   ❑ Very much! I would like to see more books by this author!
   ❑ Moderately. I would have enjoyed it more if

   _____

   _____

   _____

2. Are you a member of **Heartsong Presents**?   ❑ Yes   ❑ No
   If no, where did you purchase this book? _____

   _____

3. How would you rate, on a scale from 1 (poor) to 5 (superior), the cover design? _____

4. On a scale from 1 (poor) to 10 (superior), please rate the following elements.

   ____ Heroine   ____ Plot
   ____ Hero   ____ Inspirational theme
   ____ Setting   ____ Secondary characters

5. These characters were special because? _____

_____

_____

6. How has this book inspired your life? _____

_____

_____

7. What settings would you like to see covered in future
   Heartsong Presents books? _____

_____

_____

8. What are some inspirational themes you would like to see
   treated in future books? _____

_____

_____

9. Would you be interested in reading other **Heartsong
   Presents** titles? ❏ Yes ❏ No

10. Please check your age range:
    ❏ Under 18   ❏ 18-24
    ❏ 25-34   ❏ 35-45
    ❏ 46-55   ❏ Over 55

Name _____

Occupation _____

Address _____

City, State, Zip _____

CAROLINA
CARPENTER
Brides
4 stories in 1

Four couples find tools for building romance in a home improvement store.

Janet Benrey, Ron Benrey, Lena Nelson Dooley, and Yvonne Lehman tell the tales of couples who find each other in the midst of daily life.

Contemporary, paperback, 352 pages, 5³/₁₆" x 8"

Presents

Great Inspirational Romance at a Great Price!

Heartsong Presents books are inspirational romances in contemporary and historical settings, designed to give you an enjoyable, spirit-lifting reading experience. You can choose wonderfully written titles from some of today's best authors like Andrea Boeshaar, Wanda E. Brunstetter, Yvonne Lehman, Joyce Livingston, and many others.

When ordering quantities less than twelve, above titles are $2.97 each.
Not all titles may be available at time of order.